D1551200

LADY NITWIT

LA DAMA BOBA

Bilingual Press/Editorial Bilingüe
Spanish Golden Age Theater

Series Editors
David M. Gitlitz
Thomas Austin O'Connor

General Editor
Gary D. Keller

Managing Editor
Karen S. Van Hooft

Associate Editors
Karen M. Akins
Barbara H. Firoozye

Assistant Editor
Linda St. George Thurston

Editorial Intern
Maura Mackowski

Address:
Bilingual Press
Hispanic Research Center
Arizona State University
P.O. Box 872702
Tempe, Arizona 85287-2702
(602) 965-3867

LADY NITWIT
LA DAMA BOBA

Lope de Vega

Introduction and Translation by
William I. Oliver
late of University of California, Berkeley

Bilingual Press/Editorial Bilingüe
TEMPE, ARIZONA

©1998 by Bilingual Press/Editorial Bilingüe

All rights reserved. No part of this publication may be reproduced in any manner without permission in writing, except in the case of brief quotations embodied in critical articles and reviews.

ISBN 0-927534-74-6

Library of Congress Cataloging-in-Publication Data

Vega, Lope de, 1562-1635.
    [Dama boba. English & Spanish]
    Lady Nitwit = La dama boba / Lope de Vega ; introduction and translation by William I. Oliver.
        p.   cm.
    ISBN 0–927534–74–6 (alk. paper)
    I. Oliver, William I.   II. Title.
    PQ6459.D36   1998
    862'.3—dc21   98–13215
                                                                          CIP

PRINTED IN THE UNITED STATES OF AMERICA

Cover design by Kerry Curtis
Interior by John Wincek, Aerocraft Charter Art Svc.

Acknowledgment
The Bilingual Press gratefully acknowledges the assistance of the Program for Cultural Cooperation Between Spain's Ministry of Culture and United States Universities in making this publication possible.

Índice/Contents

☙ INTRODUCTION

1. LOPE IN THE YEAR OF *LA DAMA BOBA*

When Lope de Vega wrote La dama boba in 1613 he was fifty-one years old, and his reputation as a dramatist was at its zenith. His name had become a symbol of excellence. His private life, however, was another matter. His son, Carlos Félix, had died in 1612, and his legal but abandoned wife, Juana, sickened and died in 1613; and it must have been in that year that Lope finally decided to take holy orders, something he did in 1614. The death of his wife and son, his ecclesiastical intentions, as well as his duties as secretary to the Duke of Sessa—none of these dampened his spirit nor depressed his amatory proclivities. In fact, he was so full of himself that he flaunted the public opinion of a deeply religious society by moving in with his new mistress, the actress Jerónima de Burgos, on the day of his ordination. That Lope found time in this turbulence of events to write a play about a woman who transforms herself through the power of love from a booby into an elegant savant would seem difficult to believe. That he wrote other plays during this period is simply another measure of his economic desperation as well as the indefatigable vigor of his body and imagination. George Morley and Courtney Bruerton in their Chronology of Lope de Vega's Comedias list three plays definitely begun and finished during the year 1613—but they also estimate a total of thirty-five or thirty-six other plays in "the hopper" of Lope's mind or "in the back drawer of his desk" in the same year.

Our world has tended to view with ever increasing disdain men who are highly sexed and have many affairs. Victorians used to refer to them as "womanizers" and made the word "seducer" a term of opprobrium; in today's parlance we censure them as "machos" and "male chauvinist pigs." Such men are often simplistically dismissed as selfish persons who care for women solely as conquests or props of their sexual vanity. I don't deny that there are always some men of this inclination, but they are seldom of any interest outside of the courts. Nor do I deny that sexual vanity is a primary element of the drone psyche. There is no doubt that "young bucks" are fearfully concerned with the need to cut a "virile" figure in the eyes of the world and, for a time, may well fail to see in women anything but a source of sensuous pleasure. To such men women are important merely as conquests that add luster to their sexual renown. Thankfully, this dull-witted psychological state of affairs seldom lasts beyond middle age, unless the men are utterly insensate. As he enters middle age even the most obdurate skirt-chaser begins to weary of the arduousness of the chase. At such an existential juncture some of them begin to alter their appetites to accommodate a more rewarding interest in the "game" of the hunt;

women cease to be the mere conquests of youthful sexual frenzy or to excite short-lived and shallow infatuations—women begin to be perceived, perhaps for the first time, as individuals. It is at this stage that lotharios discover that women can matter more as persons than they ever did as mere sexual objects.

In my opinion Lope demonstrated from his earliest escapades a tendency that definitely sets him apart from these insensate whoremongers, a tendency that should earn for him a somewhat less severe judgment than one passes upon unimaginative womanizers. The truth is that Lope loved being in love as much as he loved sex. The record of his affairs would suggest that, like Stendhal, love was the passion of his life, its true object; Lope loved women in order to be in love. It may be argued, however, that loving love does not necessarily imply that one loves a person. Loving a person is far more difficult, complicated, exciting, and enduring a process than simply being in love for love's sake. A person of more modest appetites than Lope's readily discovers that loving one person for an extended period of time is quite rewarding and as difficult a challenge as human experience can tolerate. But persons in love with loving, as I suspect Lope to have been through much of his life, need to keep the temperature of their passion at such a heated level that a single love is unable to fuel the furnace of their fervor. The lover of love has many affairs not out of callousness but because he or she demands to be constantly aflame with passion and, therefore, moves from one love to the next the instant the chill of habit and familiarity settles around their hearts.

Lope loved women as sexual objects—of this there can be no question! Just examine his glancing remark from *Arte nuevo de hacer comedias* on the subject of proper presentation of women in the theater, "Let not ladies disregard their character, and if they change costumes, let it be in such a wise that it may be excused; for male disguise usually is very pleasing." Breeches roles were popular in Spain and in Italy primarily because they exhibited that portion of a woman's anatomy that the age found most exciting: the leg or thigh. Love devoid of sensuality isn't worth the mention and Lope was demonstrably a highly sexed man, but he was as much the victim of love as he was the aggressive seducer. This *monstruo de la naturaleza* was in turn devoured by a monstrous passion for love. Few men have devoted more of their lives to love than did Lope. It is the passion for love that burns and rages through his plays. It was his skill at making love that supported him economically: he undoubtedly made more money writing love letters for his patrons than he ever did by the sale and publication of his 1800 plays. Nor is it surprising that Lope, the lover, should become a priest. The ecclesiastical post earned him badly needed money, it's true, but it also gave him an opportunity to practice a different, more difficult, and perhaps "higher" kind of courtship in loving God.

Lope may have abducted women, he may have loved and left them, but he seemed loath to use them as mere sexual objects; he loved them as persons—and he loved them, as often as not, to the point of endangering his life and reputation. His plays, furthermore, are eloquent expressions of his disdain for the objectification of women: rapists, men who force themselves upon women with no motive other than sexual desire, invariably become the villains of his dramas. It is the villain's disdain for women that unfailingly draws Lope's fire. Quite simply, Lope came to love women as people because of his incurable addiction to love. It is in this fervor of love that Lope wrote about Finea, a woman whose capacity for love was a match for his own; the achievement that her love inspired was, arguably, no less great than that achieved by Lope's own inspiration.

2. *LA DAMA BOBA* IN THE CURRENT OF WOMEN'S RIGHTS

Persons uninformed about the fight for women's rights may fail to appreciate the daring of the subject of *La dama boba*. When judged by the standards of today's more strident feminist demands, the play might even appear timid; however, the historical truth of the matter is quite the opposite. It is precisely the emancipation of women that is at the very heart of this play.

Women of the medieval world had been known to rule estates while their husbands were off on crusades, but their power was ceded back upon the husband's return or upon the widow's remarriage. Of course, there have always been women who ruled through the puppet gestures of weak husbands. The liberation of women from the old patriarchal order entailed four things: (1) education, (2) economic independence, (3) relative freedom from the chores of bed, board, and children, and (4) a social situation in which men found the mobility of women desirable. Ben Jonson gives us an early picture of this movement in *Epicoene*, which depicts the ancestresses of the bluestockings. This same feminine assertion in France led to the evolution of the *salonieres,* a group of formidably intelligent and charming women whose exemplar was Madame de Staël, the only person to drive a lasting thorn into Napoleon's ego! Without the *salonieres,* the phenomenon of women such as Georges Sand and Mary Wollstonecraft could not have occurred. Spain was not as open and mobile a culture as that of France or England, countries in which upper-class women began early on to claim their rights to freedom more vigorously and openly. Certain French and English women discovered themselves to be sufficiently rich to get their way, sufficiently educated to hold their own in the company of men, and sufficiently daring to disparage the mandatory virtues of submission, motherhood, and wifeliness; but in Spain and Italy women were never allowed full rein, and there assertive women were held in a stricter bondage to the ideals of a patriarchal culture.

What Lope shows us in *La dama boba* is precisely how far these daring Spanish ladies got within the patriarchal Iberic culture of the early seventeenth century. Women here, as elsewhere, were tutored by a family retainer or a parent; upon very

rare occasions, and for obvious reasons, they were self-taught, as is Finea. Learned
women were almost all of "good" or rich families, and they were almost always
viewed as "wonders," and almost as often they were the subject of male ridicule.
Jonson, Molière, and Lope have a good time at the expense of their literary pre-
cosities in skirts, but we must not forget that they also lampooned the same verbal
and manneristic excesses in men. The skills of Lope's Finea are clearly contrasted
to the excesses of her sister Nise and her effete suitors. Molière makes the same distinctions in his portrayal of the women and their hangers-on in such plays as *Le
Misanthrope*. In each of these dramatic instances learning is the banner that heralds
female independence; but even though the best of these women were expected to
marry, there is no question about their ability to hold their own in a world of men.
Certainly no husband would be able to ignore Nise or Finea, and I doubt if any
husband would ever take them for granted.

In *La dama boba* we are given a dishearteningly accurate description of the lot of
an ideal woman of her day by none other than Finea's beleaguered father Octavio
and his friend Miseno:

OCTAVIO	Besides, I'm not attacking intelligent women; I'm simply exposing the Bacheloresses of Art. The perfect wife is made of virtue and modesty in equal parts.
MISENO	Since you don't require knowledge you'd better add, "plus a baby every year!"
OCTAVIO	Intelligence in a wife consists in just this: loving and serving her husband well, staying at home and out of the hurly burly of the world, being modest in speech and dress, earning the respect of her family, keeping her eyes and ears to herself, teaching the chil-dren, and paying more attention to her grooming than her beau-ty! What earthly use are learned conceits to a good woman?

It is one of the play's more delicious ironies that no one with any experience of the
world could believe that either Nise of Finea would ever decline into such a docile
role.

Freedom of the sort women can demand and achieve today was utterly beyond
the ken of Spanish women at the beginnings of the seventeenth century. True, certain women of the very highest station or the very lowest achieved something like
today's freedom or mobility. Some aristocratic ladies in the isolation of their estates
and within the insulation of their wealth and power could carve out for themselves
oases of freedom, but most of them would have to bend to convention and marry.
Some, like Sor Juana Inés de la Cruz, found, at least for a while, that God was a
more permissive groom than any of the real suitors in her path. There were to be
Spanish ladies such as La Duquesa de Alba who could be more or less open in her
extramarital affairs, but none could compare with the intellectual, social, and sex-

ual freedoms enjoyed by the English bluestockings or the French *salonieres*. Spanish ladies of remarkable education seemed to have no possibilities outside of marriage, relatively chaste spinsterhood, or the austerities of the veil. Of these three, marriage offered them the greatest mobility, while the veil could give their intellect full rein, but only as long as they did not soften or improvise changes on the theologically starched pleats of their veil.

Among the Spanish lower classes, some whores achieved a measure of independence when they became madams, but it must be remembered that whores had their counterparts of the demanding husband in their *bravos, alcahuetes,* or pimps. A few women escaped marriage and whoredom and became pirates or bandits living on a kind of parity with their fellow male criminals. Though this criminal element appears in some of the plays, it is generally a fallen "lady," not the hoydenish lower-class women, who interests the playwrights, and these ladies are always made to pay for their criminality and "unnatural" behavior.

Nise and Finea are both in a Portia-like situation and must find a means to circumvent their father's will; like Portia, Nise and Finea learn to cheat. Cheating becomes a virtue if only because it is the only way to cope with the father's intransigence and oppressive paternal power. Cheating in the great plays of the seventeenth century becomes a cardinal, almost the ultimate humanistic virtue; for only cheating allows men and women to get around the inhuman rigidity of laws and contracts. We need not limit our defense of cheating to Shakespeare, Lope, and Molière—as recent a genius as Brecht makes it a principal virtue of all his heroes and heroines, and for the same reasons as his seventeenth-century antecedents. The world has changed but not that much. Women may really be close to achieving a freedom comparable to that of men, but their new freedom has yet to solve the problems of child birthing and rearing. The family, which once provided the armature of social value, is presently so enfeebled as to distort the contours of our society to the point of amorphousness; and not a small part of this enfeeblement is due to the success of women's rights, which has been accompanied by an increased familial irresponsibility in the male. Societies are always in a process of change—it is their nature to change—but it would be naive to say that they change the world for the better. Where social changes are concerned, differences become their own rewards, and it would be simplistic to view them as improvements. Finea and Nise are two of the early changers who initiated the differences that are enjoyed by today's women.

3. WHO WAS LOPE DE VEGA CARPIO?

Lope's literary achievements stagger one's comprehension. What can the mind extrapolate from the fact that one man wrote well over 1800 plays in verse? The very fact seems to dehumanize the author. Add to this incomprehensibility the added achievements of having written novels, pastoral romances, epic poems, and collections of verse, and Lope's human contours seem to explode.

An attempt to define the author's humanity by examining the nonliterary events of his life stuns the imagination in a different but equally powerful manner. Lope's life was so crammed with escapades, political and artistic strife, as well as marital and amorous imbroglios that the lives of his heroes pale by comparison.

Since I can't escape a derealizing effect by either approach, I try to content myself with a mythologically enormous image; but still, the need to see Lope as an intelligible human entity nags at me. I hope that the following biographical chronology will, to some extent, shrink Lope's achievements and escapades enough to make the colossus a bit more accessible to the imagination. In order to accomplish this, I give up any attempt at a representative enumeration of Lope's known plays and focus almost exclusively on the events of his life and his non-dramatic writings. I find that his nondramatic writings serve as "teasers" that remind me of my deliberate and enormous omission. Banishing temporarily from my imagination the ghostly horde of volumes that would contain the 1800 plays in verse is the only way I have discovered to understand Lope the man.

> 1562, born in Montaña in Asturias. His father owned an embroidery workshop.

> 1574, wrote his first play, *El verdadero amante,* at age 12.

> His precocious talents brought him patronage of the Bishop Jerónimo Manrique of Ávila, later bishop of Cartagena, who got him admitted to Santiago, one of the major colleges of the University of Alcalá. The register of the period, however, does not list his name. He was never graduated and perhaps did nothing more than attend the major lectures; we can rest assured that he played the riotous student to the hilt.

> Ca. 1583, he must have spent some time in the company of actors in Madrid. He then went off on a military expedition to subdue the Azores, but he did not pursue a military career.

> Returning to Madrid, he began to write plays for a certain Velázquez, manager of a theater company and father of Elena Osorio (actress). Elena decided to seek a richer "protector" than Lope. In revenge Lope began to sell his plays to Velázquez's competitors and wrote scurrilous verses against the manager, his wife, and his daughter:

> > ¿Una dama se vende a quien la quiere
> > en almoneda está? ¿Quieren comprarla?
> > su padre es quien la vende que, aunque calla
> > su madre la sirvió de pregonera.
> >
> > Hear me young cocks! There's a lady for sale!
> > To the fleamarket hie you if you hanker to buy!

Her father awaits you, your money to take
And her mother it is who's crying her wares!

> 1588, for verses such as these, Lope was arrested and sentenced to eight years of banishment from Madrid and a two-year banishment from Castille. Two weeks before he was to leave Madrid, Lope abducted Isabel de Urbina, whose parents opposed the marriage. This crime bore the sentence of death. Lope eventually fled and sent Isabel, now pregnant, back to Madrid. Thinking that it would help his case, Lope enlisted in the Armada but won no great laurels for his service (unlike Cervantes at the battle of Lepanto).

> 1589, his marriage by proxy to Isabel expunged his sentence for abduction and he was allowed to return and reside in Valencia. He joined his wife in Valencia, where the *Corral de la Olivera* benefited from his presence.

> 1590, he was able to return to Castille and moved to Toledo, where he first served Francisco Ribera and then Diego Álvares, Duke of Alba. Living with the Duke at Alba de Tormes near Salamanca gave Lope an opportunity once again to plunge into the student life at the nearby University of Salamanca. There are accounts of several amorous escapades during this period.

> 1595, his wife, Isabel, died. His sentence of exile having expired, Lope was able to return to Madrid.

> 1598, Catherine of Savoy (Philip II's daughter) died; mourning and the intervention of a group of theologians led to a complete ban on theatrical productions. Lope needed more income; he met the Duke of Sarria (later Count of Lemos, Cervantes's patron) and became his secretary, with the special task of drafting love letters—a talent that was to become one of his major sources of income for the rest of his life.

He wrote *La Arcadia*, a pastoral novel and *La Dragoneta,* an epic poem. He paid court to Juana de Guardo, daughter of a rich wholesale grocer/butcher who provisioned much of the food of Madrid. Lope married her in 1598, but her father refused her a dowry because he disapproved of a "scribbler" for a son-in-law. Góngora made much fun of Lope over this marriage and also lampooned him (later) over his "coat of arms" with the following:

Por tu vida, Lope, que me borres
las diez y nueve torres de tu escudo
porque, aunque todas son de viento, dudo
que tengas viento para tantas torres.

'Pon your life, Lope, please erase
Those nineteen towers from your escutcheon!
They're nothing more than windmills, after all!
And you haven't got the wind to keep them up.

> 1599, three months after his marriage to Juana he began courting Micaela de Luján (a married actress). For several years after her husband left for the Americas, Micaela divided her attentions between the household of the children from her previous marriage and those she had with Lope.

> 1600, theaters reopened. Micaela went on tour and Lope followed her to Granada and Seville.

> 1602, he published *La hermosura de Angélica,* an epic poem written in 1588 while aboard the *San Juan* of the Spanish Armada.

> 1604, he produced *El peregrino en su patria,* a novel containing lists of his plays thus far published. Lope's plays were printed from 1604 to 1647 in twenty-five volumes of twelve plays each.

> 1605, Lope left the service of the duke of Sarria and entered that of the Duke of Sessa (twenty-three years old and an amateur poet). Lope remained for the rest of his life the Duke's "Secretary of Affairs of the Heart."

> 1609, he wrote *Arte nuevo de hacer comedias en este tiempo,* in which he set forth his dramatic theories, namely, (1) the three-act play: Act I = exposition; Act II = plot complication; Act III = rapid climax and conclusion. (2) Abandonment of the unities of time and place and the establishment of two- and three-plot structures. (3 Comedy and tragedy should be mingled. (4) Noble and base characters should appear in the same play. (5) Variety of verse forms appropriately applied were a good thing! *Romance:* exposition, *redondilla:* love scenes, sonnets: soliloquies, *lira:* heroic declamation. (Having set down these rules, he proceeded to ignore them, using whatever form he pleased according to the inspiration of the moment.) (6) Reveling in puns, disguises, mistaken identities. (7) Admission of all themes to drama: national, foreign, religious, heroic, pastoral, historical, contemporary, and mythological. Among Lope's favorite themes are honor, monarchy, faith, and, of course, love. (8) Use of fixed types: *galán, viejo, gracioso, pastor, bobo,* and their female counterparts.

> 1609, he also wrote *Jerusalén conquistada,* an epic poem written to rival or compete with Tasso's *Gerusalemme liberata.*

> 1610, Lope broke off relations with Micaela Luján, leaving her with several children, and moved back to Madrid where his reputation as a dramatist soared to its peak. No playwright in the history of the theater has enjoyed such fame and notoriety within his lifetime. "That's as good as Lope" meant "the very best"!

> 1612, Carlos Félix, his son, died. *Pastores de Belén,* a long pastoral romance, was published.

> 1613, his wife, Juana, died. He wrote *La dama boba.*

> 1614, with his return to the forefront of the theater world, Lope began to come to terms with the church (which in no way implies a change of

lifestyle). He became a priest, taking holy orders in Toledo and, on the day of his ordination, went to live with a new mistress, another actress, named Jerónima de Burgos, whom he had met the previous year, days before Juana's death. He published *Rimas sacras.* Lope continued to write Sessa's love letters. The scandal created by these events was such that Lope (who joined the Duke in his adventures) could not find a confessor.

> 1616, Jerónima was soon replaced by yet another actress, Lucía de Salcedo ("la Loca"), whose hold on Lope was such that he followed her to Valencia under the pretext of visiting another son, who was a monk. Thereafter he went off with Lucía on tour.

> 1616/17, he met Marta de Nevares (the "Amarilis" of his poems), twenty-six years old, married to a man as old as Lope, and mother of several children. Lope introduced himself into her household as a "spiritual guide." Marta's husband died, conveniently legitimizing Lope's bastard. However, Marta bore him two more daughters who were not only illegitimate but also, one might say, "sacrilegious" since their father continued to profess his orders and regularly said mass. Lope's fame was such that the scandal of this impious affair was condoned, and he continued to receive honors and appointments to various high offices.

Lope's fame and enormous output of plays, poems, novels, and panegyrics by no means provided him with the money necessary to support his various adventures and familial responsibilities. He had advised a son not to become a poet (the boy joined the military and was killed at sea). Lope had to beg shamefully for extra stipends from his master and companion in carousals, the Duke of Sessa, pleading to be made his private chaplain and promising to say mass for him every day for a modest fee.

> 1625, he published *Los triunfos divinos,* poetry in a Petrarchan mode.

> 1627, he wrote *La corona trágica* about Mary, Queen of Scots.

> 1628, Marta de Nevares went insane.

> 1629, he wrote *El laurel de Apolo,* a eulogy of some 300 poets.

> 1632, Marta, blind and mad, died. Of the two daughters he had by Marta (father "unknown") one took the veil (in 1621) and the other, María Antonia, lived with him as his niece and was his only joy after her mother died.

> 1632, he wrote *La Dorotea,* a long prose romance.

> 1634, Lope's daughter María Antonia, a willing victim, was abducted (but later abandoned) by Cristóbal Tenorio—carried off, as Isabel de Urbina had been by Lope himself.

> August 1635, his heart broken by María Antonia's abduction, Lope died. The familiars of the Holy Office, the Knights of St. John, and many of the priests of

Madrid carried Lope de Vega Carpio, "Phoenix of the Poets," to his grave. Lope died having sired 14 children, 7 of whom were illegitimate, and having written 1,800 *comedias* and 400 *autos sacramentales,* of which 426 *comedias* and 42 autos survive.

4. Rules and Objectives of This Translation

While working on the translation of *La dama boba,* I tried to keep the following precepts in mind:

1. Translate a comedy!

2. Be as accurate as laughter permits.

3. Endeavor to match comic effect in English for comic effect in Spanish. For instance, it is all right to change a name to preserve the gist of a jest.

4. Make all transmogrifications of the original as close to the original as comedy will allow.

5. Avoid excess language in an effort to "capture the original."

6. Do not try to write in verse; formal prose will accomplish the comic translation more economically than will verse and will lead to greater dramatic efficacy and accuracy.

7. Make the translation accessible to a contemporary audience, but avoid glaring misuse of contemporary expressions in an effort to achieve contemporaneity. The play is rooted in the values of early seventeenth-century Spain.

8. Translate for the stage, not the page.

9. Avoid editing Lope's play in the course of translation for a possible production of my own—such editing should be the responsibility of each director.

10. Make no directorial footnotes unless they are necessary to clarify the original. If there is a dramatic point to be made, however, forget the footnote and incorporate its sense into the translation. There are no footnotes in the theater.

5. Verse versus Prose

I have heard good verse translations of Golden Age plays; Roy Campbell was enough of a poet to almost bring it off, and then he did so only in the case of the serious *comedias.* I know of no translations of the comic pieces that can begin to compare with Wilbur's translations of Molière, and even Wilbur's achievements of rhyme and meter trouble me when I hear them in the theater. This may be the consequence of the English language itself. Rhyme is a devilish problem in English because we lack masculine and feminine endings comparable to the *o/a* endings of Spanish. We have an inordinate number of vowels and consonants making rhyme seem all the more unnatural. Rhyme in English has a way of announcing its artificiality so that it intrudes disruptively upon the ease of realistic dialogue. Comedy will not allow excess verbiage; the whole effect of a comic turn depends upon the propriety of its tempo, rhythm, and emphasis pattern as they coincide with the actor's movement—the achievement of rhyme and meter often leads to excessive verbiage. especially in the act of translating comic Spanish dialogue.

These reasons were enough to recommend formal prose for this translation of *La dama boba*. My choice was made even easier because much of the play's comedy emerges from the pretentious excess of *cultismo* and *conceptismo*. Translating such stuff into rhymed verse would lead to a much "fatter" or sluggish English version than the original Spanish; this had to be avoided at all costs.

Other sources of the comic in the piece, such as character and situational comedy, are really better served by prose than verse and rhyme. Finea's slow-witted reaction patterns, the maid's salty speech, the long-suffering rhythms of Octavio's paternal martyrdom, the emotional quandary of the lovers as they vacillate between courting money or pursuing wit, Finea's remarkable progress from a booby to a wit—all these were served better by the rhythmic variety and situational precision of prose.

6. VERSE FORMS OF THE ORIGINAL

Having given my reasons for not translating *La dama boba* into rhymed verse, I nevertheless want to point out the various verse forms employed by Lope in this play as a means of calling the attention of the reader who does not speak Spanish to the variety of verse forms employed by Lope. I do so because Lope himself entertained the notion that particular verse forms were suited to express specific situations.

ACT I

lines	verse forms
1-184	*redondillas*
185-272	*octavas*
273-412	*redondillas*
413-492	*romance, i-o*
493-524	*redondillas*
525-538	*soneto*

539-634	*redondillas*
635-648	*soneto*
649-888	*redondillas*
889-1062	*romance, o-a*

ACT II

1063-1154	*redondillas*
1155-1214	*quintillas*
1215-1230	*redondillas*
1231-1364	*romance, a-e*
1365-1484	*redondillas*
1485-1540	*endecasílabos sueltos y pareados*
1541-1580	*redondillas*
1581-1667	*silvas*
1668-1787	*redondillas*
1788-1824	*silvas*
1825-1860	*redondillas*
1861-2032	*romance, a-a*

ACT III

2033-2072	*quintillas*
2073-2220	*redondillas*
2221-2318	*baile y cantar con estribillos*
2319-2426	*redondillas*
2427-2634	*romance, e-o*
2635-2870	*redondillas*
2871-2930	*romance, e-e*
2931-3026	*redondillas*
3027-3184	*romance, o-a*

Redondilla: a stanza of four verses of eight syllables each, rhyming abba.

Octava: eight lines of eleven syllables, rhyming abababcc.

Silvas: a metrical combination in which, customarily, endecasyllables alternate with heptasyllables; some freely rhymed and some "paired" or consecutively rhymed (*pareados*).

Quintillas: a metrical composition in five verses of eight syllables each; employing two rhymes arranged in such a manner that the three rhymes of one are separated and so that the double verse/rhyme does not come at the end as a couplet: ababa.

Romance: a type of Spanish verse employed especially for narratives or ballads; octosyllabic, ending each second line in assonance as opposed to strict rhyme.

Lira: a combination of five verses (the first, third, and fourth heptasyllabic; the remaining two are endecasyllabic); rhymed in the manner of *quintillas.*

Terceto (tercets): a metrical combination of three endecasyllables repeated throughout a passage and ending in a cuarteto (composed of four endecasyllabic verses—when rhymed they can rhyme abba). The first and third verses of the terceto rhyme. The second verse of the terceto rhymes with the first verse of the next terceto. In the case of the sonnet, the rhyme of the two tercetos which form part of it are combined *ad libitum.*

It might be of interest for the reader to compare and contrast the arbitrary but simple rules of versification that Lope himself recommends in his *Arte nuevo de hacer comedias* against those which he employs in this play:

> Tactfully suit your verse to the subjects being treated. *Décimas* are good for complainings; the sonnet is good for those who are waiting in expectation; recitals of events ask for *romances,* though they shine brilliantly in *octavas. Tercetos* are for grave affairs and *redondillas* for affairs of love. Let rhetorical figures be brought in, as repetition or anadiplosis, and in the beginning of these same verses the various forms of anaphora; and also irony questions, apostrophes, and exclamations.

7. THE SONG AND DANCE

Few things are more dangerous for English-speaking actors than song and dance in Spanish classical drama. Such passages prove to be dramatic mine fields for any director or company that takes them for granted! The song and dance of *La dama boba* are no exception. Finea and Nise's song and dance in Act III should be an enormously effective moment within the comedy, but it must be understood and given proper attention. Fundamental to its success is the naturalness and believability of the situation within which the song and dance take place. We must not approach it as though it were an arbitrary musical interlude. Among the graces taught to Spanish women of the upper classes were singing, dancing, and some form of musicianship; these were to be displayed or deployed at family gatherings. These occasions were not, as a rule, formal trials of the women, nor were they crass exhibitions of the ladies' marital eligibility, although no father or brother would object to this musical benefit. The Spaniard understands song and dance primarily as an invitational activity.

This scene, then, is not a static recital in which the family sits by stonily while critically observing the young ladies. Everyone in the scene should become involved in the music, making it a celebration. The family and friends provide much of the percussive background for the dance and should join in on the refrains. It is possible and even desirable if some of the men in the family or from amongst the musicians were to join in the dance. Their presence in the dance would give Finea and Nise someone to "tease" in the illustrative enactment of the lyrics. This scene should be as lively, relaxed, and frolicsome as possible.

The composer for this scene (as well as any other musical interlude in Golden Age drama) must know popular Spanish music, not just as given musical forms, but as the cohesive force of a social situation. The composer must, in other words, appreciate the dramatic role of the music.

It may be pointed out that any extended song with a refrain is a tune which builds to a participational climax; if it doesn't do this, you can rest assured that you have a bad composer or a dull interpretation of the song and dance scene. One wants to provoke the "others" to join in with the dancing as well as the singing, through the refrain and the percussive accompaniment. The tune and dance should be so lively that the audience feels encouraged to join in by clapping and singing the refrain (syncopation is of the essence). In order to make this happen, one must be careful not to stage the dance and song too far away from the audience; to the contrary, the greater the intimacy the easier it will be for the actors to "warm up the house." It is even desirable for the actors and dancers, when they feel that the house is "with them," to break frame and invite them to join in the refrains.

If my suggestions seem a bit extreme, I ask the reader simply to consider the length of the song. If one is unable to approach both song and dance in the spirit that I suggest, it would be advisable to cut it from a production altogether—nothing is more lamentable than a flaccid and perfunctory musical interlude, halfheartedly inserted into a comedy.

8. THE ACTING OF LA DAMA BOBA

Reading La dama boba solely as literature seems to me to be an impossible chore; I simply cannot conceive of why one would do such a thing with this or any other good play—it is something like prizing the pulp of an orange after its juice has been extracted. All plays are meant to be imagined by their readers as theater. The difficulty for some readers arises from the fact that they have not developed the skills to read the nonverbal aspects of communication that lie imbedded in the play script. The difficulty is increased when the reader is not acquainted with the stylistic nature of the theater from another historical period.

If one were to search for stylistic analogues amid contemporary genres of theater performance, I suppose one could determine the approach to the acting in La dama boba as a hybrid between realistic musical comedy and realistic Shakespeare—the kind of thing one would expect to see in a fine production of Midsummer Night's Dream that rendered a degree of believability even unto the rustics. Actors must acquit themselves with considerable vitality and high spirits. Their performances must leap energetically beyond the proscenium and assault the imaginations of the audience; there is no place in *La dama boba* for Chekhovian inwardness. The audience should not be asked to "come to the actors," rather the actors should assault the audience and rouse it from its mental lethargy into an almost participational attention and enthusiasm.

These characters are, like most of the figures in Golden Age *comedia,* devoid of subtext; whatever information they reserve they will convey later in some form of soliloquy or aside. Yet it is important for the actors to play the psychological twists-and-turns of their characters with consummate variety, skill, and liveliness, for we have become accustomed to psychological realism with all of its subtextual colorations. If an actor abdicates his inventive responsibilities, presuming upon the language to buoy him through the play, he will soon discover how wrong he is. The reactive pattern of the actors is of cardinal importance. It is the only way to prevent the language from becoming declamation that falls upon the tympanum like hail on a zinc roof. Played imaginatively and with personal brio, the characters will satisfy any audience today.

However, the actor is not yet out of the technical woods, for he or she must address the questions of tempo and rhythmic variety: there should be no silences on the stage other than those declared by suspenseful business or reactive patterns. Actors must pick up cues with the alacrity of starved trout taking the bait, yet must take care not to set an even or mechanically rushed pace. The tempo is determined by (1) the alacrity of the author's mind, a quality he invests in (2) the minds of the characters he created, and which imaginatively infects the minds of (3) the actors in his cast, and which, finally, is reflected in (4) the tensions of the situations of his play. Readers who read slowly or with much mental rumination may miss out utterly in appreciating this vital aspect of the play's brightness of style—they do not hear its dramatic music.

Readers should also remember that actors must never rattle the "fancy" speeches. They must always invent them or if they are prepared speeches that the character has "memorized" for the occasion, they must "recall" them—by doing so, they discover the proper situational rhythms of their speeches. Rattling lines is unpardonable in any form of theater! These two psychological procedures should be part of a reader's appreciation of the script as play.

Whenever good actors, today as well as in the seventeenth century, make contact with the audience in a direct address or through song and dance sections, they do so through their character and not as performers. It is at no time wrong for an audience to see and appreciate the skill of the actors' performing; performing could and does show, but it never takes precedence over the situation within which a character finds him or herself. Today's reader must imagine favorite performers in the various roles. How, for example, would Alice Ghostly play Clara? How would a young Nancy Marchand or Meryl Streep play Nise? How would Carol Burnett play Finea? These are not idle questions; something akin to them must have run through Lope's mind during the composition of the play.

Obviously this play was written by a playwright who knew his actors. Lope wrote for well-known actors—actors known to their public but, most importantly, actors known to Lope himself. He knew what they could do and what it was that showed them off to best advantage, and this knowledge informed Lope's composition. There is certainly little doubt that Lope knew the technical abilities and qualities of the actress who played Finea. The manuscript of the play demonstrates Lope's practical or directorial concerns, for on the page listing of the cast and actors, Lope crossed out the names of three actors (those who were to play Leandro, Feniso, and Duardo) and replaced them with the names of other actors. He knew his cast—and the "María" who played Finea must have been very well known to him for her name is entered in quick and very clear lower-case letters—as though her casting were a foregone conclusion. No other actor's name is as clearly or quickly written. This information is of little consequence unless it informs one's appreciation of Lope's practical theater concerns. Above all, it is a clue to the extraliterary importance of the actress who plays Finea to the success of the production (as opposed to the script).

Finea must be played with considerable subtlety, especially in the first part of the play when she is at the most amusing level of idiocy. No greater mistake can be made than to play Finea broadly, "indicating" her dim-wittedness. This actress was expected to contribute a radioactive center to the play. Imagine, if you can, *Born Yesterday* without Judy Holliday or *The Wizard of Oz* without Judy Garland. The role of Finea should inspire directors to search for an approximation of this kind of "personality" talent. Beyond technique and good looks, the actress who plays Finea must possess a personal charm and vitality that is unique. Having left the theater, the memory of this actress should make us smile with pleasant admiration; and, I am convinced, Lope meant for her talents to be *fused* with the image of the role he had created for her. All the actors in the cast should be lively and impressive in their various roles, but the actress who plays Finea should be well nigh impossible to forget. The reader of *La dama boba* must try to get beyond Lope's words and people the stage of the script with a delightful cast of specific performers—this is the way that actors, directors, and playwrights read scripts and, I have no doubt about it, the way Lope himself composed his plays.

Lady Nitwit
La dama boba

Personajes

Liseo, *caballero*

Turín, *lacayo*

Leandro, *caballero*

Otavio, *viejo*

Miseno, *su amigo*

Laurencio, *caballero*

Duardo, *caballero*

Feniso, *caballero*

Rufino, *maestro*

Nise, *dama*

Finea, *su hermana*

Clara, *criada*

Celia, *criada*

Pedro, *lacayo*

Un maestro *de danzar*

Músicos

La escena es en Illescas y Madrid.

Characters

Liseo, *gentleman*

Turín, *Liseo's servant*

Leandro, *gentleman*

Octavio, *old man*

Miseno, *Octavio's friend*

Laurencio, *gentleman*

Duardo, *gentleman*

Feniso, *gentleman*

Rufino, *reading teacher*

Nise, *Octavio's daughter*

Finea, *her sister*

Clara, *Finea's maid*

Celia, *Nise's maid*

Pedro, *Laurencio's servant*

Dancing Master

Musicians

The scene is in Illescas and Madrid.

1

Acto Primero

Escena 1

[Portal de una posada en Illescas.]
[Liseo, caballero, y Turín, lacayo; los dos de camino]

LISEO	¡Qué lindas posadas!
TURÍN	¡Frescas!
LISEO	¿No hay calor?
TURÍN	Chinches y ropa tienen fama en toda Europa.
LISEO	¡Famoso lugar Illescas! No hay en todos los que miras quien le iguale.
TURÍN	Aun si supieses la causa . . .
LISEO	¿Cuál es?
TURÍN	Dos meses de guindas y de mentiras.

LISEO	Como aquí, Turín, se juntan
	de la Corte y de Sevilla,
	Andalucía y Castilla,
	unos a otros preguntan,
	    unos de las Indias cuentan,
	y otros con discursos largos
	de provisiones y cargos,
	cosas que el vulgo alimentan.
	    ¿No tomaste las medidas?

TURÍN	Una docena tomé.
LISEO	¿Y imágenes?
TURÍN	Con la fe que son de España admitidas, por milagrosas en todo cuanto en cualquiera ocasión les pide la devoción y el nombre.
LISEO	Pues, dese modo, lleguen las postas, y vamos.

10

20

2

 Act One

Scene 1

[Hall in an inn in Illescas.]

[Enter Liseo, a gentlemen, and Turín, a servant—both dressed as travelers.]

LISEO   What elegant inns we have in this country!

TURÍN   And so well ventilated!

LISEO   Well, we can't complain of the heat. *[He shrugs.]*

TURÍN   But bedbugs and lice can be had at any price. *[He shrugs.]*

LISEO   Yet it's a famous place, Illescas. You'd look a long time to find its equal.

TURÍN   You know the reason. . . .

LISEO   Which is?

TURÍN   Tall tales and travelers' yarns.

LISEO   Not surprising, Turín. They come here from the court, Seville, Castile, and Andalusia, and fall to boasting, some of the Indies, and others on their merchandise and cargoes; the crowd feasts on these stories and then goes off exaggerating what it's heard. Have you performed your "devotions to the Virgin"?

TURÍN   *[He holds up a bag and shakes it.]* A dozen bottles of holy water.

LISEO   And images?

TURÍN   *[Holding up another package, rattling it.]* Another dozen! They're famous throughout the kingdom! Miraculous! She'll grant whatever you ask of her.

LISEO   Well, in that case, post horse and post haste!

TURÍN   Aren't you going to eat?

Turín	¿No has de comer?
Liseo	Aguardar a que se guise es pensar que a media noche llegamos; y un desposado, Turín, ha de llegar cuando pueda lucir.
Turín	Muy atrás se queda con el repuesto Marín; pero yo traigo qué comas.
Liseo	¿Qué traes?
Turín	Ya lo verás.
Liseo	Dilo.
Turín	¡Guarda!
Liseo	Necio estás.
Turín	¿Desto pesadumbre tomas?
Liseo	Pues, para decir lo que es . . .
Turín	Hay a quien pesa de oír su nombre. Basta decir que tú lo sabrás después.
Liseo	¿Entretiénese la hambre con saber qué ha de comer?
Turín	Pues sábete que ha de ser . . .
Liseo	¡Presto!
Turín	. . . tocino fiambre.
Liseo	Pues, ¿a quién puede pesar de oír nombre tan hidalgo? Turín, si me has de dar algo, ¿qué cosa me puedes dar que tenga igual a ese nombre?
Turín	Esto y una hermosa caja.
Liseo	Dame de queso una raja; que nunca el dulce es muy hombre.
Turín	Esas liciones no son de galán ni desposado.
Liseo	Aún agora no he llegado.
Turín	Las damas de Corte son todas un fino cristal: transparentes y divinas.
Liseo	Turín, las más cristalinas comerán.

30

40

50

LISEO	If we stay for a meal, it will be midnight before we get there; and a new bridegroom, Turín, should arrive when he can shine.
TURÍN	Marín is still lagging behind with our food, but I've got a little something you might like.
LISEO	What?
TURÍN	You'll see.
LISEO	Tell me.
TURÍN	Wait!
LISEO	Stop playing the fool.
TURÍN	Scratchy today, aren't we!
LISEO	All I'm asking is . . .
TURÍN	There're some whose stomach turns at the mention of it . . . but you'll know in due time.
LISEO	My stomach takes heart in knowing that food's on its way.
TURÍN	Very well, know that it is . . .
LISEO	Presto!
TURÍN	Cold, smoked pork.
LISEO	Well, Turín, what Spaniard would complain of a fine Christian dish like that?! What could equal the lineage of "cold, smoked pork"?
TURÍN	There's that . . . and a box of candied quince!
LISEO	Sweets are for ladies. Give me cheese any day!
TURÍN	What a vulgar sentiment for a newborn swain.
LISEO	I've yet to be baptized.
TURÍN	But they say ladies of the court are different. They're as delicate as crystal—fine! transparent! and divine!
LISEO	Even the most crystalline must eat, Turín!

TURÍN	¡Es natural!	60
	Pero esta hermosa Finea	
	con quien a casarte vas	
	comerá . . .	
LISEO	Dilo.	
TURÍN	No más	
	de azúcar, maná y jalea.	
	Pasaráse una semana	
	con dos puntos en el aire,	
	de azúcar.	
LISEO	¡Gentil donaire!	
TURÍN	¿Qué piensas dar a su hermana?	
LISEO	A Nise, su hermana bella,	70
	una rosa de diamantes,	
	que así tengan los amantes	
	tales firmezas con ella;	
	y una cadena también,	
	que compite con la rosa.	
TURÍN	Dicen que es también hermosa.	
LISEO	Mi esposa parece bien,	
	si doy crédito a la fama,	
	de su hermana poco sé;	
	pero basta que me dé	
	lo que más se estima y ama.	80
TURÍN	¡Bello golpe de dinero!	
LISEO	Son cuarenta mil ducados.	
TURÍN	¡Bravo dote!	
LISEO	Si contados	
	los llego a ver, como espero.	
TURÍN	De un macho con guarniciones	
	verdes y estribos de palo,	
	se apea un hidalgo.	
LISEO	Malo,	
	si la merienda me pones!	

ESCENA II

[Leandro, de camino.—Dichos]

LEANDRO	Huésped, ¿habrá qué comer?	
LISEO	Seáis, señor, bien llegado.	90
LEANDRO	Y vos en la misma hallado.	
LISEO	¿A Madrid? . . .	

TURÍN	Goes without saying! But tell me now, this exquisite Finea you're about to marry . . . she must eat no more than . . .
LISEO	Speak up.
TURÍN	. . . sugar and spice and everything nice; going a week or more on nothing but air and a speck or two of sugar!
LISEO	Now, there's a giddy conceit!
TURÍN	What presents are you giving to her sister?
LISEO	To her lovely sister, Nise—a rose of diamonds! and, so she can bind her lovers to her, a chain of gold that competes with the rose.
TURÍN	They say she's pretty.
LISEO	If what they say is true, my bride will do well enough, thank you. I know little of the sister. It's enough that my lady give me what I crave most!
TURÍN	An avalanche of money!
LISEO	Forty thousand ducats!
TURÍN	Now that's what I call a damned good dowry!
LISEO	*If* I get my hands on it! As I hope.
TURÍN	Look, sir, there's a gentleman—of a sort—descending from a horse with wooden stirrups and a green harness.
LISEO	Hide the food 'til he's gone.

SCENE II

[Enter Leandro in traveling costume.]

LEANDRO	Well, is there food to be had hereabouts?
LISEO	Welcome, sir.
LEANDRO	Good day to you, sir.

LEANDRO	Dejéle ayer,
	cansado de no salir
	con pretensiones cansadas.
LISEO	Ésas van adjetivadas
	con esperar y sufrir.
	Holgara por ir con vos:
	lleváramos un camino.
LEANDRO	Si vais a lo que imagino,
	nunca lo permita Dios.
LISEO	No llevo qué pretender;
	a negocios hechos voy.
	¿Sois de ese lugar?
LEANDRO	Sí soy.
LISEO	Luego podréis conocer
	la persona que os nombrare.
LEANDRO	Es Madrid una talega
	de piezas, donde se anega
	cuanto su máquina pare.
	Los reyes, roques y arfiles
	conocidas casas tienen;
	los demás que van y vienen
	son como peones viles:
	todo es allí confusión.
LISEO	No es Otavio pieza vil.
LEANDRO	Si es quien yo pienso, es arfil,
	y pieza de estimación.
LISEO	Quien yo digo es padre noble
	de dos hijas.
LEANDRO	Ya sé quién;
	pero dijérades bien
	que de una palma y de un roble.
LISEO	¿Cómo?
LEANDRO	Que entrambas lo son;
	pues Nise bella es la palma;
	Finea un roble, sin alma
	y discurso de razón.
	Nise es mujer tan discreta,
	sabia, gallarda, entendida,
	cuanto Finea encogida,
	boba, indigna y imperfeta.
	Y aun pienso que oí tratar
	que la casaban . . .
LISEO	*[A Turín]* ¿No escuchas?

100

110

120

130

LISEO	On your way to Madrid?
LEANDRO	I left it yesterday, exhausted in the pursuit of exhausting petitions.
LISEO	Petitions go hand in hand with hope and suffering. I wish we were traveling together, we'd get along well.
LEANDRO	If your business is anything like mine, may God stop you.
LISEO	Oh no! I plead no petition; mine's already granted. Are you from Madrid?
LEANDRO	I am.
LISEO	Then you may know this person.
LEANDRO	Madrid's one great chess box big enough to devour all the chessmen in the world! Kings, rooks, and bishops have their appointed places, but all the others that so busily come and go are no more than pawns. It's one great madhouse, believe me.
LISEO	Certainly Octavio is no pawn.
LEANDRO	If it's the one I know, he's a rook and an important one too.
LISEO	The man I speak of is father to two daughters.
LEANDRO	Right! But you'd put it better if you distinguished between the daughters—one's a flower, the other's a weed.
LISEO	How?!
LEANDRO	No more—no less! Nise's the lovely flower; but Finea's a weed without soul or discourse of reason! Nise's as intelligent, wise, elegant, and learned a woman as Finea's insignificant, stupid, nitwitted . . . in short, im-per-fect! But despite all this I've heard it said they're going to marry her off.
LISEO	*[Aside to Turín]* Hear that?
LEANDRO	True that there're not many who could equal Finea in dowry. But pity the poor wretch who drags that beast to the altar! However, there's more than one threadbare marquis who, for want of money, courts the stupidities of this lady; they've

LEANDRO   Verdad es que no habrá muchas
           que la puedan igualar
              en el riquísimo dote;
           mas, ¡ay de aquel desdichado
           que espera una bestia al lado!
           Pues más de algún marquesote,
              a codicia del dinero,
           pretende la bobería
           desta dama, y a porfía
           hacen su calle terrero.   140

LISEO   [A Turín]
              Yo llevo lindo concierto.
           ¡A gentiles vistas voy!

TURÍN   [A Liseo]
           Disimula.

LISEO   [A Turín] Tal estoy,
           que apenas hablar acierto.—
              En fin, señor, ¿Nise es bella
           y discreta? . . .

LEANDRO   Es celebrada
           por única, y deseada,
           por las partes que hay en ella,
              de gente muy principal.

LISEO   ¿Tan necia es esa Finea?   150

LEANDRO   Mucho sentís que lo sea.

LISEO   Contemplo, de sangre igual,
              dos cosas tan desiguales . . .
           Mas, ¿cómo en dote lo son?
           Que, hermanas, fuera razón
           que los tuvieran iguales.

LEANDRO   Oigo decir que un hermano
           de su padre la dejó
           esta hacienda, porque vio
           que sin ella fuera en vano   160
              casarla con hombre igual
           de su noble nacimiento,
           supliendo el entendimiento
           con el oro.

LISEO   Él hizo mal.

LEANDRO   Antes bien, porque con esto
           tan discreta vendrá a ser
           como Nise.

TURÍN   ¿Has de comer?

LISEO   Ponme lo que dices, presto,
              aunque ya puedo escusallo.

turned the street in front of her house into a veritable lovers'
lane!

LISEO   *[To Turín]* Fine mess I'm in!

TURÍN   *[To Liseo]* Don't let on.

LISEO   *[To Turín]* Words fail me. *[To Leandro]* And so, sir, Nise . . . is
             lovely and intelligent?

LEANDRO   Unique! Her charms are highly esteemed and sought after by
             the most important people in the city!

LISEO   And is Finea . . . such an idiot?

LEANDRO   Does it bother you?

LISEO   I'm puzzled that such unequal fruit should sprout from the
             same branch. The disparity in dowry, too! Since they're sisters,
             one would think their dowries would be equal.

LEANDRO   A paternal uncle, I've heard tell, left Finea this dowry. He knew
             it would be foolish even to think of pairing her off with one of
             her own station, unless her "reason" was lined with gold!

LISEO   That's an awful thing to do!

LEANDRO   I disagree. This golden assistance will make her as wise as Nise.

TURÍN   Sir, do you feel like lunching?

LISEO   It doesn't matter now. Bring it here!

LEANDRO   May I be of further service?

LISEO   Thank you, sir, no. *[Leandro leaves.]* What a charming bride!

SCENE III

[Turin and Liseo]

TURÍN   What now?

LISEO   Mount up! I've lost my appetite.

Leandro	¿Mandáis, señor, otra cosa?	170
Liseo	Serviros. (¡Qué linda esposa!) *[Vase Leandro.]*	

Escena III

[Turín, Liseo]

Turín	¿Qué haremos?
Liseo	Ponte a caballo, que ya no quiero comer.
Turín	No te aflijas, pues no es hecho.
Liseo	Que me ha de matar, sospecho, si es necia, y propia mujer.
Turín	Como tú no digas «sí», ¿quién te puede cautivar?
Liseo	Verla no me ha de matar, aunque es basilisco en mí.
Turín	No, señor.
Liseo	También advierte que, siendo tan entendida Nise, me dará la vida, si ella me diere la muerte. *[Éntrense.]*

180

Escena IV

[Sala en casa de Otavio en Madrid.]
[Salgan Otavio, viejo, y Miseno.]

Otavio	Ésa fue la intención que tuvo Fabio.
Miseno	Parece que os quejáis.
Otavio	¡Bien mal emplea mi hermano tanta hacienda! No fue sabio. Bien es que Fabio, y que no sabio, sea.
Miseno	Si en dejaros hacienda os hizo agravio, vos propio lo juzgad.
Otavio	Dejó a Finea, a título de simple, tan gran renta, que a todos, hasta agora, nos sustenta.
Miseno	Dejóla a la que más le parecía de sus sobrinas.
Otavio	Vos andáis discreto; pues, a quien heredó su bobería, dejó su hacienda para el mismo efeto.
Miseno	De Nise la divina gallardía,

190

TURÍN	Calm down, the fat's not in the fire . . . yet.
LISEO	She'll be the death of me! Married to a nitwit! That's too much!
TURÍN	Until you say "yes," you're a free man.
LISEO	The sight of her will kill me! . . . like a basilisk!
TURÍN	I doubt it.
LISEO	On the other hand, it's possible Nise, bright as she is, will revive me—after the other has killed me.

SCENE IV

[Room in Octavio's house in Madrid.]

[Enter Octavio, an old man, and Miseno his friend.]

OCTAVIO	That was Prudencio's purpose.
MISENO	And you complain of it?
OCTAVIO	An absolutely frivolous disposition of his wealth! for a man named Prudencio! I say it even though he was my brother!
MISENO	He chose the niece that favored him most.
OCTAVIO	How discreet you've become in old age! Even though that inheritance maintains us to this day . . . I'll say it! . . . he left his estate to the one that inherited his stupidity and for no other reason.
MISENO	Nise's grace, high promises, and wit have won you over. There's no doubt you're better disposed toward her.
OCTAVIO	They are both my daughters; but I swear to you, when I try my best to show my love, each has her way of annoying and irritating me. That Finea is a simpleton is as plain as the nose on your face, but that's remedied by the dower of Fortune and a few gifts from Mother Nature who is always over-generous with beauty. But to see Nise, so haughty and learned, worshipped by that herd of fops for her well-turned phrases and

                 las altas esperanzas y el conceto
                 os deben de tener apasionado.
                 ¿Quién duda que le sois más inclinado?   200

OTAVIO   Mis hijas son entrambas; mas yo os juro
                 que me enfadan y cansan, cada una
                 por su camino, cuando más procuro
                 mostrar amor y inclinación a alguna.
                 Si ser Finea simple es caso duro,
                 ya lo suplen los bienes de Fortuna
                 y algunos que le dio Naturaleza,
                 siempre más liberal, de la belleza;
                   pero ver tan discreta y arrogante
                 a Nise, más me pudre y martiriza,   210
                 y que de bien hablada y elegante
                 el vulgazo la aprueba y soleniza.
                 Si me casara agora (y no te espante
                 esta opinión, que alguno lo autoriza),
                 de dos extremos: boba o bachillera,
                 de la boba elección, sin duda, hiciera.

MISENO   ¡No digáis tal, por Dios!; que están sujetas
                 a no acertar en nada.

OTAVIO   Eso es engaño;
                 que yo no trato aquí de las discretas:
                 sólo a las bachilleras desengaño.   220
                 De una casada son partes perfetas
                 virtud y honestidad.

MISENO   Parir cadaño,
                 no dijérades mal, si es argumento
                 de que vos no queréis entendimiento.

OTAVIO   Está la discreción de una casada
                 en amar y servir a su marido;
                 en vivir recogida y recatada,
                 honesta en el hablar y en el vestido;
                 en ser de la familia respetada,
                 en retirar la vista y el oído,   230
                 en enseñar los hijos, cuidadosa,
                 preciada más de limpia que de hermosa.
                   ¿Para qué quiero yo que, bachillera,
                 la que es propia mujer concetos diga?
                 Esto de Nise por casar me altera;
                 lo más, como lo menos, me fatiga.
                 Resuélvome en dos cosas que quisiera,
                 pues la virtud es bien que el medio siga:
                 que Finea supiera más que sabe,
                 y Nise menos.

MISENO   Habláis cuerdo y grave.   240

elegant speech, turns my bile and annoys me even more. If I were getting married right now—now don't be amazed, for I know whereof I speak—of the two extremes, booby or the lady scholar, I would without batting an eyelash, pick the booby!

MISENO   For God's sake, don't talk like that! Boobies are doomed to make a muddle of everything they touch!

OCTAVIO   That's hearsay. Besides, I'm not attacking intelligent women; I'm simply exposing the Bacheloresses of Art. The perfect wife is made of virtue and modesty in equal parts.

MISENO   Since you don't require knowledge you'd better add, "plus a baby every year!"

OCTAVIO   Intelligence in a wife consists in just this: loving and serving her husband well, staying at home and out of the hurly burly of the world, being modest in speech and dress, earning the respect of her family, keeping her eyes and ears to herself, teaching the children, and paying more attention to her grooming than her beauty! What earthly use are learned conceits to a good woman? Getting Nise married off troubles me! The excess in one annoys me as much as the lack in the other. Since virtue always seeks the mean, I long but for two things: that Finea knew more than she does . . . and Nise, far less!

MISENO   True enough!

OCTAVIO   No doubt of it! Since all extremes are bad, I've cause for discontent.

MISENO   And what news of your future son-in-law?

OCTAVIO   Ah, yes. Really, the duties of a father give one pause! I get Finea married off, a notable indication of our reverence for gold! While Nise, wise, learned, and knowledgeable, can scarcely find a suitor; yet Finea's suitors, suitors of gold more than wit, and their relatives as well, hound me every minute of the day!

MISENO   You must admit, there's a "quantity" of reasons for her popularity.

OTAVIO   Si todos los extremos tienen vicio,
              yo estoy, con justa causa, discontento.

MISENO   Y, ¿qué hay de vuestro yerno?

OTAVIO   Aquí el oficio
              de padre y dueño alarga el pensamiento:
              caso a Finea, que es notable indicio
              de las leyes del mundo, al oro atento.
              Nise, tan sabia, docta y entendida,
              apenas halla un hombre que la pida;
                  y por Finea, simple, por instantes
              me solicitan tantos pretendientes   250
              —del oro más que del ingenio amantes—,
              que me cansan amigos y parientes.

MISENO   Razones hay, al parecer, bastantes.

OTAVIO   Una hallo yo, sin muchas aparentes,
              y es el buscar un hombre en todo estado,
              lo que le falta más, con más cuidado.

MISENO   Eso no entiendo bien.

OTAVIO   Estadme atento.
              Ningún hombre nacido a pensar viene
              que le falta, Miseno, entendimiento,
              y con esto no busca lo que tiene.   260
              Ve que el oro le falta y el sustento,
              y piensa que buscalle le conviene,
              pues como ser la falta el oro entienda,
              deja el entendimiento y busca hacienda.

MISENO   ¡Piedad del cielo, que ningún nacido
              se queje de faltarle entendimiento!

OTAVIO   Pues a muchos, que nunca lo han creído,
              les falta, y son sus obras argumento.

MISENO   Nise es aquesta.

OTAVIO   Quítame el sentido
              su desvanecimiento.

MISENO   Un casamiento   270
              os traigo yo.

OTAVIO   Casémosla; que temo
              alguna necedad, de tanto estremo.   *[Vanse.]*

ESCENA V

[Nise y Celia, criada]

NISE   ¿Dióte el libro?

CELIA   Y tal, que obliga

OCTAVIO   I know only one explanation: every man, regardless of station, takes great pains to seek what he lacks most!

MISENO   I don't follow.

OCTAVIO   No man born of woman, Miseno, believes that he lacks learning and good sense and, since he thinks he needs them not, he seeks them not. However, it's quite apparent to him that he lacks money and so he sets out to seek it! The minute he feels a pinch on his purse, he leaves learning in the lurch and chases after gold.

MISENO   When men begin to lament their good sense, God have mercy on Spain!

OCTAVIO   Believe me, many who never doubt their good sense, lack it— their deeds are proof enough.

MISENO   Here comes Nise.

OCTAVIO   Her giddy logic makes me dizzy!

MISENO   I bring her a proposal of marriage.

OCTAVIO   Quick, let's get her married, for heaven's sake! Her extremes I'm afraid will lead to no good end.

SCENE V

[Octavio and Miseno leave; Nise enters with Celia, a maid.]

NISE   Did he give you the book?

CELIA   It was all I could do to touch it, much less open it!

NISE   Why, for heavens sake?!

CELIA   I didn't want to soil it! The cover of the book, of white vellum no less, was decorated with all manner of golden flowers!

NISE   And well he merits them! Heliodorus! Greek poet divine!

CELIA   Looks like prose to me.

	a no abrille ni tocalle.	
NISE	Pues, ¿por qué?	
CELIA	Por no ensucialle,	
	si quieres que te lo diga.	
	En cándido pergamino	
	vienen muchas flores de oro.	
NISE	Bien lo merece Eliodoro,	
	griego poeta divino.	280
CELIA	¿Poeta? Pues parecióme	
	prosa.	
NISE	También hay poesía	
	en prosa.	
CELIA	No lo sabía.	
	Miré el principio, y cansóme.	
NISE	Es que no se da a entender,	
	con el artificio griego,	
	hasta el quinto libro, y luego	
	todo se viene a saber	
	cuanto precede a los cuatro.	
CELIA	En fin, ¿es poeta en prosa?	290
NISE	Y de una historia amorosa	
	digna de aplauso y teatro.	
	Hay dos prosas diferentes:	
	poética y historial.	
	La historial, lisa y leal,	
	cuenta verdades patentes,	
	con frase y términos claros;	
	la poética es hermosa,	
	varia, culta, licenciosa,	
	y escura aun a ingenios raros.	300
	Tiene mil exornaciones	
	y retóricas figuras.	
CELIA	Pues, ¿de cosas tan escuras	
	juzgan tantos?	
NISE	No le pones,	
	Celia, pequeña objeción;	
	pero así corre el engaño	
	del mundo.	

ESCENA VI

[Finea, dama, con unas cartillas, y Rufino, maestro.—Dichas]

FINEA	¡Ni en todo el año	
	saldré con esa lición!	

NISE   There is poetry in prose.

CELIA   You don't say! I just glanced at the beginning and I'm worn out!

NISE   Greek artifice! It won't reveal itself until you've read the fifth book. Then, of course, everything that has transpired in the first four becomes absolutely clear.

CELIA   And so he's a poet in prose?

NISE   And of an amorous history worthy of applause—in the theater! There are two kinds of prose, Celia, poetical and historical. The historical, plain and verisimilitudinous, reveals patent truths in clear terms and phrases. The poetical is lovely, varied, cultured, licentiously free, dark even to the gaze of rare geniuses, and it's invested with thousands of embellishments and rhetorical figures!

CELIA   Well, how can so many people understand such dark subjects?

NISE   That's no small criticism, dear Celia, but . . . it's the way the world deceives itself.

SCENE VI

[Finea enters carrying some ABC cards. She is followed by her tutor Rufino.]

FINEA   I could study a whole year and never get this lesson!

CELIA   *[To Nise]* Your sister and her teacher.

NISE   Has she learned her alphabet?

CELIA   She's still struggling over *A*.

RUFINO   Be patient or I won't show you any more letters. Now what's this?

FINEA   It must be a letter.

RUFINO   Letter?

FINEA   Something else?

CELIA	*[Aparte a Nise]* Tu hermana, con su maestro.
NISE	¿Conoce las letras ya? 310
CELIA	En los principios está.
RUFINO	¡Paciencia y no letras muestro! ¿Qué es ésta?
FINEA	Letra será.
RUFINO	¿Letra?
FINEA	Pues, ¿es otra cosa?
RUFINO	*[Aparte]* No, sino el alba. (¡Qué hermosa bestia!)
FINEA	Bien, bien. Sí, ya, ya; el alba debe de ser, cuando andaba entre las coles.
RUFINO	Ésta es *ca.* Los españoles no la solemos poner 320 en nuestra lengua jamás. Úsanla mucho alemanes y flamencos.
FINEA	¡Qué galanes van todos estos detrás!
RUFINO	Éstas son letras también.
FINEA	¿Tantas hay?
RUFINO	Veintitrés son.
FINEA	Ah[o]ra vaya de lición; que yo lo diré muy bien.
RUFINO	¿Qué es ésta?
FINEA	¿Aquesta? . . . No sé.
RUFINO	¿Y ésta?
FINEA	No sé qué responda. 330
RUFINO	¿Y ésta?
FINEA	¿Cuál? ¿Esta redonda? ¡Letra!
RUFINO	¡Bien!
FINEA	Luego, ¿acerté?
RUFINO	¡Linda bestia!
FINEA	¡Así, así! Bestia, ¡por Dios!, se llamaba; pero no se me acordaba.
RUFINO	Ésta es *erre,* y ésta es *i.*

RUFINO	No, no! It's not a letter! . . . it's *E! E!* . . . for e-le-phant!! *[Aside]* What a gorgeous beast!
FINEA	All right, all right! So it isn't an elephant! It's a letter. Right? But what's it doing with its tail?!
RUFINO	This is *K*. We Spaniards never use it but the Germans and Flemish use it often.
FINEA	And look at all the other cards! Aren't they pretty!
RUFINO	These are all letters.
FINEA	That many!
RUFINO	Twenty-three of them!
FINEA	Well! Let's get on with the lesson. You'll see how well I do.
RUFINO	What is this?
FINEA	That one? I don't know.
RUFINO	And this one?
FINEA	Haven't the slightest.
RUFINO	And this?
FINEA	The little round one?
RUFINO	Well?
FINEA	Well what?
RUFINO	Booby! You exquisite booby!
FINEA	Oh, that's it! Booby! That's what it's called! I'd forgotten.
RUFINO	This is *O!* . . . and this is *U!*
FINEA	Me?
NISE	What a muddle!
RUFINO	Now, repeat after me: *C-O-M-E*—come.
FINEA	Where?
RUFINO	God deliver me!

FINEA	Pues, ¿si tú lo traes errado . . . ?
NISE	(¡Con qué pesadumbre están!)
RUFINO	Di aquí: *b, a, n: ban.*
FINEA	¿Dónde van?
RUFINO	¡Gentil cuidado!
FINEA	¿Que se van, no me decías?
RUFINO	Letras son; ¡míralas bien!
FINEA	Ya miro.
RUFINO	*B, e, n: ben.*
FINEA	¿Adónde?
RUFINO	¡Adonde en mis días no te vuelva más a ver!
FINEA	¿*Ven,* no dices? Pues ya voy.
RUFINO	¡Perdiendo el jüicio estoy! ¡Es imposible aprender! ¡Vive Dios, que te he de dar una palmeta!
FINEA	¿Tú a mí?
RUFINO	¡Muestra la mano! *[Saca una palmatoria.]*
FINEA	Hela aquí.
RUFINO	¡Aprende a deletrear!
FINEA	¡Ay, perro! ¿Aquesto es palmeta?
RUFINO	¡Pues, ¿qué pensabas?
FINEA	¡Aguarda! . . .
NISE	¡Ella le mata!
CELIA	Ya tarda tu favor, Nise discreta.
RUFINO	¡Ay, que me mata!
NISE	¿Qué es esto? ¿A tu maestro?
FINEA	Hame dado causa.
NISE	¿Cómo?
FINEA	Hame engañado.
RUFINO	¿Yo engañado?
NISE	¡Dila presto!
FINEA	Estaba aprendiendo aquí la letra *bestia* y la *ca* . . .

340

350

360

FINEA   You told me to come, didn't you?

RUFINO   These—are—letters! Look at them!

FINEA   All right.

RUFINO   G-O—go!

FINEA   Where?

RUFINO   Where I will never again in all my days set eyes on you!

FINEA   You tell me to go, I go.

RUFINO   I'm losing my mind! It's impossible to teach you anything! By God, there's nothing for it! I'm going to give you a caning!

FINEA   Aren't you sweet!

RUFINO   [Rufino produces a ruler.] Give me your hand.

FINEA   Oh my! Here.

RUFINO   Now, learn to say your ABCs! [He slaps her across the hand.]

FINEA   Ow! You dog! So that's what a caning is!

RUFINO   Of course!

FINEA   Waaatch ooouut! [She charges him and knocks him down.]

NISE   She's killing him!

CELIA   Nise, my dear, the time has come to set aside your modesty . . . your intervention is long overdue.

RUFINO   Help! She's killing me!

NISE   What's the meaning of this? . . . and your teacher too!

FINEA   He started it.

NISE   What!

FINEA   He tricked me!

RUFINO   I?!

NISE   Out with it.

NISE   La primera sabes ya.

FINEA   Es verdad: ya la aprendí.
                 Sacó un zoquete de palo
            y al cabo una media bola;
            pidióme la mano sola
            (¡mira qué lindo regalo!),
                 y apenas me la tomó,
            cuando, ¡zas!, la bola asienta,   370
            que pica como pimienta,
            y la mano me quebró.

NISE   Cuando el discípulo ignora,
            tiene el maestro licencia
            de castigar.

FINEA   ¡Linda ciencia!

RUFINO   Aunque me diese, señora,
                 vuestro padre cuanto tiene,
            no he de darle otra lición.   *[Vase.]*

ESCENA VII

CELIA   ¡Fuese!

NISE   No tienes razón:
            sufrir y aprender conviene.   380

FINEA   Pues, ¿las letras que allí están,
            yo no las aprendo bien?
            Vengo cuando dice *ven*,
            y voy cuando dice *van*.
                 ¿Qué quiere, Nise, el maestro,
            quebrándome la cabeza
            con *ban, bin, bon*?

CELIA   *[Aparte]*   ¡Ella es pieza
            de rey!

NISE   Quiere el padre nuestro
                 que aprendamos.

FINEA   Ya yo sé
            el Padrenuestro.

NISE   No digo   390
            sino el nuestro; y el castigo,
            por darte memoria fue.

FINEA   Póngame un hilo en el dedo
            y no aquel palo en la palma.

CELIA   Mas que se te sale el alma.
            Si lo sabe . . .

FINEA   I was learning my letters, and I'd learned the letter "booby" and the letter "elephant" . . .

NISE   No need to teach you the first of those, I'm sure.

FINEA   You're right, I know that one well! . . . and so, he took out a ruler with a little knob on the end of it, and then he asked me to put out my hand. A fine present he made me! He took my hand and, WHACK! . . . hit me with the stick! It stung worse than pepper and nearly broke my hand in two.

NISE   When the pupil is inattentive the teacher is obliged to punish her.

FINEA   Fine thing that is!

RUFINO   M'lady, even though your father were to give me everything he possesses! . . . I would never, ever give her another lesson! *[Rufino leaves.]*

Scene VII

CELIA   There goes another one!

NISE   My dear, you are not reasonable; it behooves you to suffer and learn.

FINEA   I learned those letters, didn't I?! I came when it said "come" and I went when it said "go." He scrambled my brains with all his comings and goings.

CELIA   *[Aside]* She's a masterpiece!

NISE   That we should learn and improve ourselves is the wish of our father who . . .

FINEA   Oh! I know! "Our Father who art in . . ."

NISE   No! No, I mean our father! . . . and you were punished only to improve your memory.

FINEA   Then let him tie a string on my finger instead of whacking my hand!

FINEA   ¡Muerta quedo!
            ¡Oh Celia! No se lo digas,
            y verás qué te daré.

Escena VIII

[Clara, criada.—Dichas]

CLARA   *[A Finea]*
            ¡Topé contigo, a la fe!

NISE   Ya, Celia, las dos amigas   400
                se han juntado.

CELIA   A nadie quiere
            más, en todas las criadas.

CLARA   ¡Dame albricias, tan bien dadas
            como el suceso requiere!

FINEA   Pues, ¿de qué son?

CLARA   Ya parió
            nuestra gata la romana.

FINEA   ¿Cierto, cierto?

CLARA   Esta mañana.

FINEA   ¿Parió en el tejado?

CLARA   No.

FINEA   Pues, ¿dónde?

CLARA   En el aposento;
            que cierto se echó de ver   410
            su entendimiento.

FINEA   Es mujer
            notable.

CLARA   Escucha un momento.
                Salía, por donde suele,
            el Sol, muy galán y rico,
            con la librea del rey,
            colorado y amarillo;
            andaban los carretones
            quitándole el romadizo
            que da la noche a Madrid,
            aunque no sé quién me dijo   420
            que era la calle Mayor
            el soldado más antiguo,
            pues nunca el mayor de Flandes
            presentó tantos servicios;
            pregonaban aguardiente,

CELIA	If your father ever found out about this, you might just as well give up the ghost!
FINEA	Now you're trying to frighten me! Oh, Celia, don't tell him! You'll see, I'll give you . . .

SCENE VIII

[Clara, a servant, enters.]

CLARA	*[To Finea]* Oh, here you are! Ran into you at last!
NISE	Look, Celia, the girlfriends have already knocked their heads together!
CELIA	Clara's her favorite of all the maids!
CLARA	Give me greetings worthy of my tidings!
FINEA	Well, what are they, Clara?
CLARA	Our tabby cat has had her kittens!
FINEA	Really?! Do you mean it?!
CLARA	This morning!
FINEA	Where? On the roof?
CLARA	No!
FINEA	Well, where then?!
CLARA	In the bedroom! . . . which goes to show how smart she is!
FINEA	Oh, she's such a lady!
CLARA	Just listen! The sun rose in its usual place, rich and handsome in the red and gold colors of the king's livery. Slop carts went rumbling through the streets of Madrid clearing out the catarrh of the night. I can't recall who it was described the main street of Madrid as one long runny nose flowing with the phlegm of many a chamber pot. The carnival revelers

agua biznieta del vino,
los hombres Carnestolendas,
todos naranjas y gritos.
Dormían las rentas grandes,
despertaban los oficios,   430
tocaban los boticarios
su almireces a pino,
cuando la gata de casa
comenzó, con mil suspiros,
a decir: «¡Ay, ay, ay, ay!
¡Que quiero parir, marido!»
Levantóse Hociquimocho,
y fue corriendo a decirlo
a sus parientes y deudos;
que deben de ser moriscos,   440
porque el lenguaje que hablaban,
en tiple de monacillos,
si no es jerigonza entre ellos,
no es español, ni latino.
Vino una gata vïuda,
con blanco y negro vestido
—sospecho que era su agüela—,
gorda y compuesta de hocico;
y, si lo que arrastra honra,
como dicen los antiguos,   450
tan honrada es por la cola
como otros por sus oficios.
Trújole cierta manteca,
desayunóse y previno
en qué recibir el parto.
Hubo temerarios gritos;
no es burla; parió seis gatos
tan remendados y lindos,
que pudieran, a ser pías,
llevar el coche más rico.   460
Regocijados bajaron
de los tejados vecinos,
caballetes y terrados,
todos los deudos y amigos:
Lamicola, Arañizaldo,
Marfuz, Marramao, Micilo,
Tumba[h]ollín, Mico, Miturrio,
Rabicorto, Zapaquildo;
unos vestidos de pardo,
otros de blanco vestidos,   470
y otros con forros de martas,
en cueras y capotillos.

and the brandy peddlers—brandy, great granddaughter of wine—both went through the street, vulgar, shouting or hawking their wares. The rich were sound asleep but the tradesmen were up and about. Apothecaries clanged their brass mortars. When all of a sudden our lady pussy cat began to cry out, "Oh! My, my, my, my! Husband, I'm in labor!" So Lopnose got up and went running to tell his relatives and kin, who must be Moorish because of the language they speak—like the screeching of so many acolytes in the treble clef—if it isn't double talk to them, is certainly not Spanish or Latin. Then came a certain widow pussy cat, dressed all in black and white. I suspect it was her grandmother. Fat she was, with a puffy muzzle; and if, as the ancients used to say, "Whatever drags upon the ground is a sign of honor," is true, then she was as honorable by virtue of her tail as many have become by their accomplishments. She brought our lady pussycat an ointment, had breakfast, and then made everything ready for the delivery. There were terrible shouts! Having kittens is no joke! But she had six of the loveliest little kittens that, had they been piebald horses, would have been worthy of drawing the most elegant of coaches. Then neighbors, friends, and relatives all came happily down from the rooftops: Lickertail, Scratchypaws, Fuzzydown, Messypad, Stubbytail, and Saucerface! Some were dressed in gray, others in white, some wore capes and jackets or cloaks of marten. Tom Glutton came to the feast in mourning clothes, in memory of the caticide of his father. Here one brings her blood pudding, another fish, another a little bit of goat meat, another a wily sparrow, and still another a simple pigeon. When I left, the representatives to this assembly of felines were planning to amuse themselves by chasing a greased mouse. Come along! When you hear them, you'll swear they sound just like children. And you must give your good wishes to the little kittens!

FINEA   Nothing could make me happier!

CLARA   Let's go!

FINEA   Lead the way!   *[Finea and Clara leave.]*

De negro vino a la fiesta
el gallardo Golosino,
luto que mostraba entonces
de su padre el gaticidio.
Cuál la morcilla presenta,
cuál el pez, cuál el cabrito,
cuál el gorrïón astuto,
cuál el simple palomino.   480
Trazando quedan agora,
para mayor regocijo
en el gatesco senado
correr gansos cinco a cinco.
Ven presto, qui si los oyes,
dirás que parecen niños,
y darás a la parida
el parabién de los hijos.

FINEA   ¡No me pudieras contar
caso, para el gusto mío,   490
de mayor contentamiento!

CLARA   Camina.

FINEA   Tras ti camino.

                    [Vanse Finea y Clara.]

ESCENA IX

NISE   ¿Hay locura semejante?

CELIA   ¿Y Clara es boba también?

NISE   Por eso la quiere bien.

CELIA   La semejanza es bastante;
               aunque yo pienso que Clara
          es más bellaca que boba.

NISE   Con esto la engaña y roba.

ESCENA X

[Duardo, Feniso, Laurencio, caballeros.—Dichas]

DUARDO   Aquí, como estrella clara,   500
               a su hermosura nos guía.

FENISO   Y aun es del sol su luz pura.

LAURENCIO ¡Oh reina de la hermosura!

DUARDO   ¡Oh Nise!

FENISO   ¡Oh señora mía!

NISE   Caballeros . . .

SCENE IX

NISE   Have you ever beheld such lunacy?

CELIA   Is Clara a nitwit too?

NISE   That's why she likes her so.

CELIA   There is a resemblance; though I feel that Clara is wittingly
            twitty.

NISE   The better to fool her and pilfer.

SCENE X

[Enter Duardo, Feniso, Laurencio—all gentlemen.]

DUARDO   Like a shining star, her beauty leads us hither!

FENISO   Shining with a light as pure as the sun's!

LAURENCIO   Oh, queen of loveliness!

DUARDO   Oh, Nise!

FENISO   Oh, m'lady!

NISE   Gentlemen.

LAURENCIO   Because of your consummate talent, we proclaim you now
            judge over Duardo's poem.

NISE   I, Finea's sister, a judge?

LAURENCIO   You and you alone! The sibyl of Spain! Not the sibyl of Cumae
            or Erythrae, but you only! You, who raise the graces to four and
            the muses to ten, you only are worthy of judging.

NISE   If you sought judgment upon mean, unworthy works, your
            election would be justified.

FENISO   Your rare discretion, impossible to praise, was justly elected; lis-
            ten, lady, to Duardo's poem.

LAURENCIO   Esta vez,
                 por vuestro ingenio gallardo,
                 de un soneto de Düardo
                 os hemos de hacer jüez.

NISE   ¿A mí, que soy de Finea
                 hermana y sangre?

LAURENCIO   A vos sola,   510
                 que sois sibila española,
                 no Cumana ni Eritrea;
                    a vos, por quien ya las Gracias
                 son cuatro, y las Musas diez,
                 es justo haceros jüez.

NISE   Si ignorancias, si desgracias
                    trujérades a juzgar,
                 era justa la elección.

FENISO   Vuestra rara discreción,
                 imposible de alabar,   520
                    fue justamente elegida.
                 Oíd, señora, a Eduardo.

NISE   ¡Vaya el soneto! Ya aguardo,
                 aunque, de indigna, corrida.

DUARDO   La calidad elementar resiste
                 mi amor, que a la virtud celeste aspira,
                 y en las mentes angélicas se mira,
                 donde la idea del calor consiste.
                    No ya como elemento el fuego viste
                 el alma, cuyo vuelo al sol admira;   530
                 que de inferiores mundos se retira,
                 adonde el serafín ardiendo asiste.
                    No puede elementar fuego abrasarme.
                 La virtud celestial que vivifica,
                 envidia el verme a la suprema alzarme;
                    que donde el fuego angélico me aplica,
                 ¿cómo podrá mortal poder tocarme,
                 que eterno y fin contradición implica?

NISE   Ni una palabra entendí.

DUARDO   Pues en parte se leyera   540
                 que más de alguno dijera
                 por arrogancia: «Yo sí.»
                    La intención, o el argumento,
                 es pintar a quien ya llega
                 libre del amor, que ciega
                 con luz del entendimiento,
                    a la alta contemplación

NISE   Bring on the poem! I'll hear it, though distressed by my
                unworthiness.

DUARDO   My love resists the elemental heat
                    and aspires to the azure virtue,
                    seeing its image in angelic minds,
                    where the very concept of heat exists,
                Fire, no longer an element,
                    garbs the soul whose flight the sun admires;
                    the soul in flight retreats from lesser worlds
                    to where the seraphim ardently assist.
                Elemental flame no longer burns me!
                    Life-giving and celestial, virtue
                    envies seeing me reach the heights supreme!
                For there, enveloped in angelic flame,
                    can mortal power touch me,
                    who, eternal and incontrovertible, resist?

NISE   I didn't understand a word.

DUARDO   Pretentiousness would have led some others to claim they did.
                But, really, it must be read first! The gist or theme is to paint
                that soul who, free of love, which blinds reason with its light,
                achieves the high contemplation of pure love-without-end
                which is fire to the seraphim.

NISE   Gist and theme are clear enough.

LAURENCIO Profound conceits!

FENISO   And they certainly disguise the theme!

DUARDO   Three fires, lovely Nise, which correspond to three worlds, pro-
                vide a principle for the other ones.

NISE   You could say that.

DUARDO   Elemental heat is the warmth within each of us; celestial heat is
                that virtue which relieves and renews us; and the angelic is the
                very idea of heat.

NISE   I lose patience with what I do not understand!

DUARDO   The element within us is fire . . .

de aquel puro amor sin fin,
donde es fuego el serafín.

NISE   Argumento y intención   550
    queda entendido.

LAURENCIO   ¡Profundos
conceptos!

NISE   ¡Mucho le esconden!

DUARDO   Tres fuegos, que corresponden,
hermosa, Nise, a tres mundos,
    dan fundamento a los otros.

NISE   ¡Bien los podéis declarar!

DUARDO   Calidad elementar
es el calor en nosotros;
    la celestial, es virtud
que calienta y que recrea,   560
y la angélica es la idea
del calor.

NISE   Con inquietud
escucho lo que no entiendo.

DUARDO   El elemento en nosotros
es fuego.

NISE   ¿Entiendéis vosotros?

DUARDO   El puro sol que estáis viendo
    en el cielo, fuego es,
y fuego el entendimiento
seráfico; pero siento
que así difieren los tres: 570
    que el que elementar se llama,
abrasa cuando se aplica;
el celeste vivifica,
y el sobreceleste ama.

NISE   No discurras, por tu vida;
vete a escuelas.

DUARDO   Donde estás,
lo son.

NISE   Yo no escucho más,
de no entenderte corrida.
    ¡Escribe fácil!

DUARDO   Platón,
a lo que en cosas divinas   580
escribió, puso cortinas
que, tales como estás, son
    matemáticas figuras
y enigmas.

NISE   Do you gentlemen understand this?

DUARDO   The pure sun which you behold in the sky is composed of fire,
            and fire is the substance of seraphic understanding. But I
            believe the three differ in the following way: The elemental is
            flame and burns when it is applied, the celestial vivifies, and
            the super-celestial . . . loves!

NISE   Upon your life, hold your tongue and go back to school!

DUARDO   School is where you are.

NISE   I won't listen to another word I cannot understand! Write
            simply!

DUARDO   When writing of divine topics Plato drew a curtain around
            them that, like my style, was composed of mathematical figures
            and enigmas.

NISE   Oh, Laurencio.

FENISO   *[To Duardo.]* That's silenced you, all right!

DUARDO   She's intimidated by dark subjects.

FENISO   Well, she is a woman.

DUARDO   But I suppose there's something to it. Written or spoken, clarity
            is appreciated by "the majority."

NISE   *[To Laurencio]* You seem in good spirits.

LAURENCIO   Since they're lodged in your heart.

NISE   I pay you well for their keep. But please don't bring along those
            persons who eclipse my talking to you thus.

LAURENCIO   M'lady, I scarce dare to stand before you, lest your radiant eyes
            like Phoebus's rays take offense at the sight of such unworthi-
            ness; but if you choose to look beyond, into my soul, you will
            find it rich in the faith of love.

NISE   I have a letter, but how can I give it to you unseen by those
            gentlemen?

NISE   ¡Oye, Laurencio!

FENISO   *[A Duardo]*
                Ella os ha puesto silencio.

DUARDO   Temió las cosas escuras.

FENISO   ¡Es mujer!

DUARDO   La claridad
                a todos es agradable,
                que se escriba o que se hable.

NISE   *[Aparte]*
                ¿Cómo va de voluntad?   590

LAURENCIO   Como quien la tiene en ti.

NISE   Yo te la pago muy bien.
                No traigas contigo quien
                me eclipse el hablarte ansí.

LAURENCIO   Yo, señora, no me atrevo,
                por mi humildad, a tus ojos;
                que, dando en viles despojos,
                se afrenta el rayo de Febo;
                    pero, si quieres pasar
                al alma, hallarásla rica   600
                de la fe que amor publica.

NISE   Un papel te quiero dar;
                    pero, ¿cómo podrá ser
                que destos visto no sea?

LAURENCIO   Si en lo que el alma desea
                me quieres favorecer,
                    mano y papel podré aquí
                asir juntos, atrevido,
                como finjas que has caído.

NISE   ¡Jesús! *[Hace Nise como que cae.]*

LAURENCIO   ¿Qué es eso?

NISE   ¡Caí!   610

LAURENCIO   Con las obras respondiste.

NISE   Ésas responden mejor,
                que no hay sin obras amor.

LAURENCIO   Amor en obras consiste.

NISE   Laurencio mío, adiós queda.
                Düardo y Feniso, adiós.

DUARDO   Que tanta ventura a vos
                como hermosura os conceda.

                                [Vanse Nise y Celia.]

LAURENCIO　If you wish to give my soul its boon let's join hand to paper; pretend to fall.

NISE　　　　Oh, my God! *[She falls.]*

LAURENCIO　What?!

NISE　　　　I fell.

LAURENCIO　You answer me in deeds!

NISE　　　　Love speaks best in deeds.

LAURENCIO　And action is the language of love.

NISE　　　　Laurencio, dear, go with God. Duardo, Feniso, good-bye.

DUARDO　　God grant you as much good fortune as he has beauty.

[Exit Nise and Celia.]

SCENE XI

DUARDO　　What did Nise tell you of the poem?

LAURENCIO　She said it was "extreme."

DUARDO　　Judging by the razor of your satires, I'll wager your comments had a cutting edge.

LAURENCIO　One need not write verses in order to cut others down; since it appears that one can censure them without understanding.

FENISO　　We have things to do! By your leave.

DUARDO　　Rather than disturb, *we* will observe the rules of decorum!

LAURENCIO　There's a sound of malice to that.

FENISO　　Not at all! The heavenly Nise is yours, or at least she seemed to be so.

LAURENCIO　That might be, were I worthy of her.

ESCENA XI

DUARDO   *[A Laurencio]*
     ¿Qué os ha dicho del soneto
Nise?

LAURENCIO   Que es muy extremado.   620

DUARDO   Habréis los dos murmurado,
que hacéis versos, en efeto.

LAURENCIO   Ya no es menester hacellos
para saber murmurallos;
que se atreve a censurallos
quien no se atreve a entendellos.

FENISO   Los dos tenemos que hacer.
Licencia nos podéis dar.

DUARDO   Las leyes de no estorbar
queremos obedecer.   630

LAURENCIO   ¡Malicia es esa!

FENISO   ¡No es tal!
La divina Nise es vuestra,
o, por lo menos, lo muestra.

LAURENCIO Pudiera, a tener igual.

ESCENA XII

[Despídanse, y quede solo Laurencio.]

LAURENCIO   Hermoso sois, sin duda, pensamiento,
y, aunque honesto también, con ser hermoso,
si es calidad del bien ser provechoso,
una parte de tres que os falta siento.
   Nise, con un divino entendimiento,
os enriquece de un amor dichoso;   640
mas sois de dueño pobre, y es forzoso
que en la necesidad falte el contento.
   Si el oro es blanco y centro del descanso,
y el descanso del gusto, yo os prometo
que tarda el navegar con viento manso.
   Pensamiento, mudemos de sujeto;
si voy necio tras vos, y en ir me canso,
cuando vengáis tras mí, seréis discreto.

ESCENA XIII

[Entre Pedro, lacayo de Laurencio.]

PEDRO   ¡Qué necio andaba en buscarte
fuera de aqueste lugar!   650

SCENE XII

[They take their leave and Laurencio remains alone.]

LAURENCIO   A happy thought! And as honest as it's lovely! But if it is a quality of virtue to seek one's profit, I find you, thought of mine, lacking one of three essential traits. Nise, with heavenly understanding, endows you with bountiful love. Nonetheless, thought of mine, you serve a penniless mistress, and there's no joy in poverty. If gold is the target of comfort, and comfort the goal of pleasure, why then my thought, your sails will be blown by a timid breeze and your voyage will be a long one. So, thought, let's change mistresses! If I foolishly persist in following you, I'll tire along the way; but if you change and follow me, you'll certainly be wiser!

SCENE XIII

[Enter Pedro, Laurencio's lackey.]

PEDRO   I was a fool to expect to find you somewhere else!

LAURENCIO   You could find my heart elsewhere.

PEDRO   Which means that you are here and she is not?

LAURENCIO   A thought has set itself in motion, within and without me. Have you noticed how the hand of a clock is fixed forever in one spot yet never seems to be at rest? Now it points at one o'clock and, later, points at two. So also with my heart, for without budging from this house, it has since it loved Nise swung high to twelve o'clock, the hour for the breaking of fasts.

PEDRO   How is this a change, pray tell.

LAURENCIO   Like the hour hand, I begin by pointing at one, and swing a full circle. I used to point toward Nise.

PEDRO   Yes . . .

LAURENCIO   Well, now I face Finea.

LAURENCIO   Bien me pudieras hallar
            con el alma en otra parte.

PEDRO   Luego, ¿estás sin ella aquí?

LAURENCIO   Ha podido un pensamiento
            reducir su movimiento
            desde mí, fuera de mí.
                ¿No has visto que la saeta
            del reloj en un lugar
            firme siempre suele estar
            aunque nunca está quïeta,   660
                y tal vez está en la una,
            y luego en las dos está?
            Pues, así mi alma ya,
            sin hacer mundaza alguna
                de la casa en que me ves,
            desde Nise que ha querido,
            a las doce se ha subido,
            que es número de interés.

PEDRO   Pues, ¿cómo es esa mudanza?

LAURENCIO   Como la saeta soy,   670
            que desde la una voy
            por lo que el círculo alcanza.
                ¿Señalaba a Nise?

PEDRO   Sí.

LAURENCIO   Pues ya señalo en Finea.

PEDRO   ¿Eso quieres que te crea?

LAURENCIO   ¿Por qué no, si hay causa?

PEDRO   Di.

LAURENCIO   Nise es una sola hermosa,
            Finea las doce son:
            hora de más bendición,
            más descansada y copiosa.   680
                En las doce el oficial
            descansa, y bástale ser
            hora entonces de comer,
            tan precisa y natural.
                Quiero decir que Finea
            hora de sustento es,
            cuyo descanso ya ves
            cuánto el hombre le desea.
                Denme, pues, las doce a mí,
            que soy pobre, con mujer   690
            que, dándome de comer,
            es la mejor para mí.

PEDRO   You don't expect me to believe that!?

LAURENCIO   Why not, if the cause is good?

PEDRO   I'm all ears!

LAURENCIO   Lovely Nise is one, alone. Finea is more like twelve—twelve
                    o'clock, an hour of blessed rest and plenty. At twelve, the
                    workman sets aside his chores; it is the natural time of day for
                    eating. What I mean is that Finea is the hour of sustenance
                    whose repose is sought by many a man. Give me twelve
                    o'clock any day, I'm poor! And the woman who'll keep me fed
                    is the one for me. Nise is an unfortunate hour in which my
                    planet stares at me with a frown. Finea is a blessed hour in
                    which my Jupiter smiles with a pleasing aspect. By courting
                    Finea, I'll be laying my hands on forty thousand ducats. From
                    this day forth, my dear Pedro, I devote myself to this under-
                    taking.

PEDRO   One reservation.

LAURENCIO   What?

PEDRO   The woman is so stupid you're bound to regret it.

LAURENCIO   Have you ever known anyone who regretted having food to eat,
                    time for rest, and clothes to put on his back? Well, she'll bring
                    this bounty with her.

PEDRO   You couldn't possibly exchange the wise and lovely Nise for an
                    ignorant nitwit!

LAURENCIO   What do you mean ignorant, you nincompoop! The sun of
                    gold outshines the sun of wit! The poor man is always stupid,
                    the rich man is always wise. There is no blemish of birth or
                    lineage that money will not repair; but the smallest imperfec-
                    tion is laid bare and magnified by poverty. From this day
                    forth, I will woo Finea!

PEDRO   Nevertheless, I suspect that, knock as loud as you will, you'll
                    open no doors in the wall of her stupidity.

LAURENCIO   I know of one.

PEDRO   Damned if I do.

     Nise es [ah]ora infortunada,
donde mi planeta airado,
de sextil y de cuadrado
me mira con frente armada.
     Finea es [ah]ora dichosa,
donde Júpiter benigno
me está mirando de trino,
con aspecto y faz hermosa.   700
     Doyme a entender que, poniendo
en Finea mis cuidados,
a cuarenta mil ducados
las manos voy previniendo.
     Ésta, Pedro, desde hoy
ha de ser empresa mía.

PEDRO   Para probar tu osadía,
en una sospecha estoy.

LAURENCIO   ¿Cuál?

PEDRO   Que te has de arrepentir
por ser simple esta mujer.   710

LAURENCIO   ¿Quién has visto de comer,
de descansar y vestir
    arrepentido jamás?
Pues esto viene con ella.

PEDRO   A Nise, discreta y bella,
Laurencio, ¿dejar podrás
    por una boba inorante?

LAURENCIO   ¡Qué inorante majadero!
¿No ves que el sol del dinero
va del ingenio adelante?   720
     El que es pobre, ése es tenido
por simple; el rico, por sabio.
No hay en el nacer agravio,
por notable que haya sido,
    que el dinero no lo encubra;
ni hay falta en naturaleza
que con la mucha pobreza
no se aumente y se descubra.
     Desde hoy quiero enamorar
a Finea.

PEDRO   He sospechado   730
que a un ingenio tan cerrado
no hay puerta por donde entrar.

LAURENCIO   Yo sé cuál.

PEDRO   ¡Yo no, por Dios!

LAURENCIO   Clara, her nitwit maid.

PEDRO   You'll find her more wily than witless.

LAURENCIO   All the better. I propose for the two of us to woo the two of
            them.

PEDRO   Clara will prove an easy bawd.

LAURENCIO   In that case my hopes are insured.

SCENE XIV

[Enter Finea and Clara.]

PEDRO   Here they come. Don't let on!

LAURENCIO   See if I can't take her in hand!

PEDRO   Nothing like trying to rouse love in a mule!

LAURENCIO   Lovely face! Fine figure!

PEDRO   Would her soul were their equal.

LAURENCIO   Now, my lovely lady, I admit that the sun does not necessarily
            rise in the East, for your eyes project much rosier rays and
            pyramidal lights. But if you blind me so at your rising, what in
            heaven's name, will you do at midday?

FINEA   Eat lunch! And not of pyramids and those silly things you talk
            of but good healthy food.

LAURENCIO   Those limpid morning stars utterly transport me! I'm not myself!

FINEA   Well, if you go wandering around when the stars are out, it's no
            wonder you catch cold. Go to bed at a decent hour and always
            wear a night cap.

LAURENCIO   Don't you understand?! I love you! Honestly . . . purely . . .
            plainly . . . without guile!

FINEA   What's love?

Laurencio	Clara, su boba criada.
Pedro	Sospecho que es más taimada que boba.
Laurencio	Demos los dos en enamorarlas.
Pedro	Creo que Clara será tercera más fácil.
Laurencio	De esa manera, seguro va mi deseo.
Pedro	Ellas vienen; disimula.
Laurencio	Si puede ser en mi mano.
Pedro	¡Que ha de poder un cristiano enamorar una mula!
Laurencio	Linda cara y talle tiene.
Pedro	¡Así fuera el alma!

740

Escena XIV

[Finea y Clara.—Dichos]

Laurencio	Agora conozco, hermosa señora, que no solamente viene el sol de las orientales partes, pues de vuestros ojos sale con rayos más rojos y luces piramidales; pero si, cuando salís tan grande fuerza traéis, al mediodía, ¿qué haréis?
Finea	Comer, como vos decís, no pirámides ni peros, sino cosas provechosas.
Laurencio	Esas estrellas hermosas, esos nocturnos luceros me tienen fuera de mí.
Finea	Si vos andáis con estrellas, ¿qué mucho que os traigan ellas arromadizado ansí? Acostaos siempre temprano, y dormid con tocador.
Laurencio	¿No entendéis que os tengo amor puro, honesto, limpio y llano?

750

760

LAURENCIO   Love? Desire.

FINEA   Of what?

LAURENCIO   Of a lovely thing.

FINEA   Pretty things like gold and diamonds?

LAURENCIO   No! Rather, beauty such as yours which is created, as God ordained it, for a happy purpose. This beauty of yours has certainly roused my desire!

FINEA   And I? What do I do . . . knowing you desire me?

LAURENCIO   Love me in return. Haven't you heard that love begets love?

FINEA   Well . . . never having been in love I don't know how it's done; I've never read about it in any of my primers, and Mother didn't teach me. I'll ask my father!

LAURENCIO   Wait! That's not the way.

FINEA   How then?

LAURENCIO   Warmed by the fire of my blood, such vivid rays will dart from my eyes, that they'll plunge like spirits into yours!

FINEA   Spirits! Oh, no! I want nothing to do with ghosts!

LAURENCIO   These spirits are ours—our own! And once joined they will burn with a sweet flame that will deprive us of peace until our souls find their way to that enviable position which is the just repose of all marriages. This holy purpose vindicates our love. What soul I have is going to rest within your breast!

FINEA   All that! And marriage too!?

PEDRO   [To Clara] Just as he, I'm struck so to the death by the love of you: I take this opportunity to . . .

CLARA   Love—what is it? I'm not sure I know.

PEDRO   Love? Madness, fury!

CLARA   You want to drive me crazy?

FINEA   ¿Qué es amor?

LAURENCIO   ¿Amor? Deseo.

FINEA   ¿De qué?

LAURENCIO   De una cosa hermosa.   770

FINEA   ¿Es oro? ¿Es diamante? ¿Es cosa
             destas que muy lindas veo?

LAURENCIO   No; sino de la hermosura
             de una mujer como vos,
             que, como lo ordena Dios,
             para buen fin se procura;
                 y ésta, que vos la tenéis,
             engendra deseo en mí.

FINEA   Y yo, ¿qué he de hacer aquí,
             si sé que vos me queréis?   780

LAURENCIO   Quererme. ¿No habéis oído
             que amor con amor se paga?

FINEA   No sé yo cómo se haga,
             porque nunca yo he querido,
                 ni en la cartilla lo vi,
             ni me lo enseñó mi madre.
             Preguntarélo a mi padre . . .

LAURENCIO   Esperaos, que no es ansí.

FINEA   Pues, ¿cómo?

LAURENCIO   Destos mis ojos   790
             saldrán unos rayos vivos,
             como espíritus visivos,
             de sangre y de fuego rojos,
                 que se entrarán por los vuestros.

FINEA   No, señor; arriedro vaya
             cosa en que espíritus haya.

LAURENCIO   Son los espíritus nuestros,
                 que juntos se han de encender
             y causar un dulce fuego
             con que se pierde el sosiego,
             hasta que se viene a ver   800
                 el alma en la posesión,
             que es el fin del casamiento;
             que con este santo intento
             justos los amores son,
                 porque el alma que yo tengo
             a vuestro pecho se pasa.

FINEA   ¿Tanto pasa quien se casa?

PEDRO With a sweet madness for which a man will exchange the highest wisdom.

CLARA Well, I'll follow my mistress's example, that's what.

PEDRO The meanest peasant can master the science of love in one, maybe two easy lessons, and once in love his will is seized with a pleasant disease.

CLARA Well, don't wish it on me! I haven't been sick a day in my life, except for chilblains.

FINEA I like your lessons!

LAURENCIO You'll see how my love will teach you . . . love is the lamp of understanding!

FINEA I like that part about getting married and positions and all.

LAURENCIO So do I.

FINEA And you'll take me off to your home and keep me there?

LAURENCIO Yes, m'lady.

FINEA And that's proper?

LAURENCIO Very, for those who marry. Your father and mother were married in this fashion, and that's how you were born.

FINEA I was?

LAURENCIO Yes.

FINEA Do you mean to say, when my father got married, I wasn't there?

LAURENCIO *[Aside]* Has there ever been such ignorance! My good fortune may drive me mad!

FINEA My father is coming!

LAURENCIO Then I must go. Remember me.

FINEA With pleasure. *[Laurencio leaves.]*

CLARA He's gone.

PEDRO   *[A Clara]*
            Con él, como os digo, vengo
                tan muerto por vuestro amor,
            que aquesta ocasión busqué.   810

CLARA   ¿Qué es amor, que no lo sé?

PEDRO   ¿Amor? ¡Locura, furor!

CLARA   Pues, ¿loca tengo de estar?

PEDRO   Es una dulce locura,
            por quien la mayor cordura
            suelen los hombres trocar.

CLARA   Yo, lo que mi ama hiciere,
            eso haré.

PEDRO   Ciencia es amor,
            que el más rudo labrador
            a pocos cursos la adquiere.   820
                En comenzando a querer,
            enferma la voluntad
            de una dulce enfermedad.

CLARA   No me la mandes tener;
                que no he tenido en mi vida
            sino solos sabañones.

FINEA   ¡Agrádanme las liciones!

LAURENCIO   Tú verás, de mí, querida,
                cómo has de quererme aquí;
            que es luz del entendimiento   830
            amor.

FINEA   Lo del casamiento
            me cuadra.

LAURENCIO   Y me importa a mí.

FINEA   Pues, ¿llevaráme a su casa
            y tendráme allá también?

LAURENCIO   Sí, señora.

FINEA   Y, ¿eso es bien?

LAURENCIO   Y muy justo en quien se casa.
                Vuestro padre y vuestra madre
            casados fueron ansí:
            deso nacistes.

FINEA   ¿Yo?

LAURENCIO   Sí.

FINEA   Cuando se casó mi padre,   840
                ¿no estaba yo allí tampoco?

PEDRO   Yes, and I must follow. Keep me in mind, hmm?

CLARA   How can I, if you leave me?   *[Pedro leaves.]*

SCENE XV

FINEA   So that's what love is all about! Who would have thought!

CLARA   Like chicken soup at a country inn, stir around long enough, and you'll eventually find the whole hen.

FINEA   My father, as you know, can be most annoying. He's tried to marry me off to a man from the Indies, or Seville, or Toledo, or some such place. He's spoken of it twice now; and this last time he brought out a little card with a picture painted on it, all polished and shiny. And when I looked at the picture, he said, "There, Finea, is your husband." And then he went away. And since, at the time, I didn't know anything about getting married, I accepted this good-for-nothing husband who's nothing more than a face, jacket, and a cloak! But Clara, what does it matter how prettily painted he is, if he has no body from the waist down? You don't see anyone walking around this house without legs, do you?

CLARA   Heavens, no! Do you have him there?

FINEA   *[Takes out the miniature.]* There he is.

CLARA   A nice face and a good figure!

FINEA   But it's lopped off at the waist!

CLARA   Well then, he won't do. But what pretty little eyes he has!

FINEA   My father and Nise!

CLARA   Is he coming to marry you off?

FINEA   There'll be no marrying this one, don't worry! For the one who just left me has legs and a body to boot!

CLARA   What's more, he hunts his quarry with dogs! His hound of a lackey has already bitten me!

LAURENCIO   *[Aparte]*
            ¿Hay semejante ignorancia?
            Sospecho que esta ganancia
            camina a volverme loco.

FINEA   Mi padre pienso que viene.

LAURENCIO   Pues voyme. Acordaos de mí.   *[Vase.]*

FINEA   ¡Que me place!

CLARA   ¿Fuese?

PEDRO   Sí,
            y seguirle me conviene.
                Tenedme en vuestra memoria.   *[Vase.]*

CLARA   Si os vais, ¿cómo?

Escena XV

FINEA   ¿Has visto, Clara,   850
            lo que es amor? ¡Quién pensara
            tal cosa!

CLARA   No hay pepitoria
            que tenga más menudencias
            de manos tripas y pies.

FINEA   Mi padre, como lo ves,
            anda en mil impertinencias.
                Tratado me ha de casar
            con un caballero indiano,
            sevillano o toledano.
            Dos veces me vino a hablar,   860
                y esta postrera sacó
            de una carta un naipecito
            muy repulido y bonito,
            y luego que le miró
                me dijo: «Toma, Finea,
            ése es tu marido.» Y fuese.
            Yo, como, en fin, no supiese
            esto de casar qué sea,
                tomé el negro del marido,
            que no tiene más de cara,   870
            cuera y ropilla; mas, Clara,
            ¿qué importa que sea pulido
                este marido o quien es,
            si todo el cuerpo no pasa
            de la pretina? Que en casa
            ninguno sin piernas ves.

CLARA   ¡Pardiez, que tienes razón!
            ¿Tiénesle ahí?

SCENE XVI

[Enter Octavio and Nise.]

OCTAVIO   They say he entered the city on horse by Toledo Street.

NISE   He should be here by now.

OCTAVIO   He has some things to settle, no doubt. I'm trembling in my
            shoes over Finea.

NISE   And there, sir, is the blushing bride.

OCTAVIO   Daughter, do you know . . .

NISE   She knows nothing! That's the sum of her misfortune.

OCTAVIO   Your husband-to-be is now in Madrid!

FINEA   What a memory! Don't you remember, you already gave him to
            me on a card!

OCTAVIO   That was just his likeness in a painting. He'll soon be here in
            the flesh.

SCENE XVII

[Enter Celia.]

CELIA   Señor Liseo has arrived. He's dismounting from his horse at this
            very moment.

OCTAVIO   Finea, look to it! Behave prudently and like a lady! Let's have
            some chairs and pillows.

SCENE XVIII

[Enter Liseo, Turín, and Servants.]

LISEO   I hope you will excuse this liberty in one who is to become
            your son.

FINEA	Vesle aquí.

[Saca un retrato.]

CLARA	¡Buena cara y cuerpo!	
FINEA	Sí;	880
	mas no pasa del jubón.	
CLARA	Luego éste no podrá andar.	
	¡Ay, los ojitos que tiene!	
FINEA	Señor, con Nise . . .	
CLARA	¿Si viene	
	a casarte . . . ?	
FINEA	No hay casar;	
	que éste que se va de aquí	
	tiene piernas, tiene traza.	
CLARA	Y más, que con perro caza;	
	que el mozo me muerde a mí.	

Escena XVI

[Entre Otavio con Nise.—Dichas]

OTAVIO	Por la calle de Toledo	
	dicen que entró por la posta.	890
NISE	Pues, ¿cómo no llega ya?	
OTAVIO	Algo, por dicha, acomoda.	
	Temblando estoy de Finea.	
NISE	Aquí está, señor, la novia.	
OTAVIO	Hija, ¿no sabes?	
NISE	No sabe;	
	que ésa es su desdicha toda.	
OTAVIO	Ya está en Madrid tu marido.	
FINEA	Siempre tu memoria es poca.	
	¿No me lo diste en un naipe?	
OTAVIO	Ésa es la figura sola,	900
	que estaba en él retratado;	
	que lo vivo viene agora.	

Escena XVII

[Entre Celia.—Dichos]

CELIA	Aquí está el señor Liseo,
	apeado de unas postas.

Octavio	And who honors us with his presence.
Liseo	Now, sir, tell me, which of the two is my bride?
Finea	Can't you tell? I am!
Liseo	Come to my arms.
Finea	Is it all right?
Octavio	Yes, yes, of course.
Finea	Clara . . .
Clara	M'lady?
Finea	He looks better with legs and feet, doesn't he?
Clara	It may be some sort of trick!
Finea	But seeing him only from the waist up bothered me a great deal more.
Octavio	Embrace your sister-in-law.
Liseo	The fame of your beauty was no lie.
Nise	Your servant.
Liseo	All Spain stands in awe of your learning. They call you "Nise, divine" for you're as wise as you are lovely. And you are lovely in extreme!
Finea	Look at the way he flirts with her! And he's come to marry me! Now, I call that rude!
Octavio	Quiet, you booby! Children, be seated, for heaven's sake.
Liseo	Turín.
Turín	Sir?
Liseo	Pretty but stupid.
Octavio	How was your journey?
Liseo	Tiresome, for eagerness has a way of lengthening a journey.

| OTAVIO | Mira, Finea, que estés
muy prudente y muy señora.
Llegad sillas y almohadas. | |

Escena XVIII

[Liseo, Turín y Criados.—Dichos]

LISEO	Esta licencia se toma quien viene a ser hijo vuestro.	
OTAVIO	Y quien viene a darnos honra.	910
LISEO	Agora, señor, decidme: ¿Quién es de las dos mi esposa?	
FINEA	¡Yo! ¿No lo ve?	
LISEO	Bien merezco los brazos.	
FINEA	Luego, ¿no importa?	
OTAVIO	Bien le puedes abrazar.	
FINEA	¡Clara . . . !	
CLARA	¡Señora . . . !	
FINEA	¡Aún agora viene con piernas y pies!	
CLARA	Esto, ¿es burla o jerigonza?	
FINEA	El verle de medio arriba me daba mayor congoja.	920
OTAVIO	Abrazad vuestra cuñada.	
LISEO	No fue la fama engañosa, que hablaba en vuestra hermosura.	
NISE	Soy muy vuestra servidora.	
LISEO	¡Lo que es el entendimiento! A toda España alborota. La divina Nise os llaman; sois discreta como hermosa, y hermosa con mucho estremo.	
FINEA	Pues, ¿cómo requiebra a esotra, si viene a ser mi marido? ¿No es más necio?	930
OTAVIO	¡Calla, loca! Sentaos, hijos, por mi vida.	
LISEO	¡Turín . . . !	
TURÍN	¿Señor?	

FINEA   You should have taken the old nag from the treadmill. She rides so smoothly you'd think you were walking.

NISE   Sister, hold your tongue.

FINEA   Be quiet yourself!

NISE   Though beautiful and virtuous, Finea's quite a little prankster!

LISEO   Turín, do you have the jewels?

TURÍN   Our things have not yet arrived.

LISEO   We have to overlook the mistakes of the servants when we travel!

FINEA   Are you giving us jewels?!

TURÍN   [Aside] Bits and bridles are the jewels for her!

OCTAVIO   You must be warm. May I get you something? What's wrong? Don't you feel well?

LISEO   Water . . . could I have some water?

OCTAVIO   On an empty stomach water might do you harm. Some candied fruits as well?

FINEA   Oh, if you'd only come last Saturday, Clara and I baked a tripe and giblet pie that . . .

OCTAVIO   Silly girl, will you be still!

FINEA   . . . and with lots of spices! Oh, it was so good! [She laughs.]

[Enter Servants with water, towel, and a box of candied fruits.]

CELIA   Have some water!

OCTAVIO   Some sweets!

LISEO   Her laughter, sir, is something to behold! Enough to drive a man to drink! . . . water, that is!   [Liseo drinks.]

FINEA   He drinks like a mule!

LISEO	*[Aparte]* ¡Linda tonta!	
OTAVIO	¿Cómo venís del camino?	
LISEO	Con los deseos enoja; que siempre le hacen más largo.	
FINEA	Ese macho de la noria pudiérais haber pedido, que anda como una persona.	940
NISE	Calla, hermana.	
FINEA	Callad vos.	
NISE	Aunque hermosa y virtüosa, es Finea de este humor.	
LISEO	Turín, ¿trajiste las joyas?	
TURÍN	No ha llegado nuestra gente.	
LISEO	¡Qué de olvidos se perdonan en un camino a criados!	
FINEA	¿Joyas traéis?	
TURÍN	*[Aparte]* Y le sobra de las joyas el principio, tanto el jo se le acomoda.	950
OTAVIO	Calor traéis. ¿Queréis algo? ¿Qué os aflige?, ¿qué os congoja?	
LISEO	Agua quisiera pedir.	
OTAVIO	Haráos mal el agua sola. Traigan una caja.	
FINEA	A fe que si, como viene agora, fuera el sábado pasado, que hicimos yo y esa moza un menudo . . .	
OTAVIO	¡Calla, necia!	
FINEA	. . . mucha especia, ¡linda cosa! *[Entren con agua, toalla, salva y una caja.]*	960
CELIA	El agua está aquí.	
OTAVIO	Comed.	
LISEO	El verla, señor, provoca; porque con su risa dice que la beba y que no coma. *[Beba.]*	
FINEA	Él bebe como una mula.	
TURÍN	*[Aparte]* ¡Buen requiebro!	

TURÍN	*[Aside]* Now, there's a compliment for you!
OCTAVIO	You are outdoing yourself today! Will you be quiet!
FINEA	Drained it to the last drop! Here, let me dry your beard!
OCTAVIO	What are you doing?!
FINEA	Who cares?
LISEO	*[Aside]* She almost pulled my beard out by the roots! Now, there's a winsome wench!
OCTAVIO	You need to rest, sir! I'll take Finea with me and give you an opportunity to compose yourself.
LISEO	*[Aside]* It's a little late to recover my composure now I'm trapped!
OCTAVIO	Go ahead you two and make his room ready.
FINEA	There's room for two in my bed.
NISE	Good God! Don't you know, you're not married yet?!
FINEA	What difference does that make?
NISE	Come along!
FINEA	In there?
NISE	Yes!
FINEA	All right. Good-bye. Anchors away!
LISEO	*[Aside]* Anchors away? Uh! If only I could! But I'm anchored to this rock of stupidity!
OCTAVIO	I, too, must go, my son, and begin the preparations for your wedding feast. God keep you.
	[Octavio, Nise, Finea, Celia, and Clara leave.]
LISEO	*[Aside]* And may He protect me and get me out of this! Woe is me!

Otavio	¡Qué enfadosa que estás hoy! ¡Calla, si quieres!
Finea	¡Aun no habéis dejado gota! Esperad; os limpiaré.
Otavio	Pues, ¿tú le limpias?
Finea	¿Qué importa?

970

Liseo	*[Aparte]* ¡Media barba me ha quitado! ¡Lindamente me enamora!
Otavio	Que descanséis es razón. *[Aparte]* Quiero, pues no se reporta, llevarle de aquí a Finea.
Liseo	*[Aparte]* Tarde el descanso se cobra, que en tal desdicha se pierde.
Otavio	Ahora bien; entrad vosotras, y aderezad su aposento.

Finea	Mi cama pienso que sobra para los dos.

980

Nise	¿Tú no ves que no están hechas las bodas?
Finea	Pues, ¿qué importa?
Nise	Ven conmigo.
Finea	¿Allá dentro?
Nise	Sí.
Finea	Adiós. ¡Hola!
Liseo	*[Aparte]* Las del mar de mi desdicha me anegan entre sus ondas.
Otavio	Yo también, hijo, me voy, para prevenir las cosas, que, para que os desposéis con más aplauso, me tocan. Dios os guarde.

990

[Todos se van; queden Liseo y Turín.]

Escena XIX

Liseo	No sé yo de qué manera disponga mi desventura. ¡Ay de mí!

SCENE XIX

[Liseo and Turín are left alone.]

TURÍN   Do you want to take off your boots?

LISEO   I want to take my life! What a frightful idiot!

TURÍN   How could heaven plant such a crazy soul in such a heavenly body.

LISEO   Even if we were already married, I could have it annulled in self defense! The law is absolutely clear on that point! Having contracted to marry a woman of good sense, they plan to marry me to a packhorse!

TURÍN   The wedding is off, I take it.

LISEO   Devil take a dowry that must be won with such toil and torture! Granted, the woman is young and lovely, but what offspring will I get by her but lynxes, lions, and tigers!?

TURÍN   That's not necessarily true. Life and literature tell us of thousands of children who dishonor their wise parents by being fools.

LISEO   Cicero did sire Marcus, who was no better than a horse! Worse! . . . a camel!

TURÍN   By the same token, foolish parents have been known to produce a phoenix.

LISEO   But we've got to admit that, as a rule, children resemble their parents. No! I'll break my word! Tear up contracts! Cross off signatures! No treasure can pay the price of freedom. But if it were Nise . . .

TURÍN   You just gave yourself away! Ha! An angry man, when he sees his image in a mirror, regains control of himself and his passion abates. And just so, when you saw your pleasure reflected in the sister's face—for pleasure is the face of your soul—you tempered your anger!

LISEO   Well said, Turín. She alone can quell the anger her father has aroused in me.

TURÍN	¿Quieres quitarte las botas?	
LISEO	No, Turín; sino la vida. ¿Hay boba tan espantosa?	
TURÍN	Lástima me ha dado a mí, considerando que ponga en un cuerpo tan hermoso el cielo un alma tan loca.	1000
LISEO	Aunque estuviera casado por poder, en causa propia me pudiera descasar. La ley es llana y notoria; pues concertando mujer con sentido, me desposan con una bestia del campo, con una villana tosca.	
TURÍN	Luego, ¿no te casarás?	
LISEO	¡Mal haya la hacienda toda que con tal pensión se adquiere, que con tal censo se toma! Demás que aquesta mujer, si bien es hermosa y moza, ¿qué puede parir de mí sino tigres, leones y onzas?	1010
TURÍN	Eso es engaño, que vemos por experiencias y historias, mil hijos de padres sabios, que de necios los deshonran.	1020
LISEO	Verdad es que Cicerón tuvo a Marco Tulio en Roma, que era un caballo, un camello.	
TURÍN	De la misma suerte consta que de necios padres suele salir una fénix sola.	
LISEO	Turín, por lo general, y es consecuencia forzosa, lo semejante se engendra. Hoy la palabra se rompa; rásguense cartas y firmas; que ningún tesoro compra la libertad. Aun si fuera Nise . . .	1030
TURÍN	¡Oh, qué bien te reportas! Dicen que si a un hombre airado, que colérico se arroja,	

TURÍN   But what of the other one? The sister?

LISEO   Would you have me trade life for death, day for night, birds for
          snakes, roses for thorns, and an angel for a demon?

TURÍN   That makes sense, and some to spare. Gold and pleasure are *not*
          necessarily synonymous, are they?

LISEO   I proclaim it! I hereby renounce the lady nitwit!

End of Act I—*Lady Nitwit*

le pusiesen un espejo,
en mirando en él la sombra
que representa su cara,
se tiempla y desapasiona;   1040
así tú, como tu gusto
miraste en su hermana hermosa
—que el gusto es cara del alma,
pues su libertad se nombra—,
luego templaste la tuya.

LISEO   Bien dices, porque ella sola
el enojo de su padre,
que, como ves, me alborota,
me puede quitar, Turín.

TURÍN   ¿Que no hay que tratar de esotra?   1050

LISEO   Pues, ¿he de dejar la vida
por la muerte temerosa,
y por la noche enlutada
el sol que los cielos dora,
por los áspides las aves,
por las espinas las rosas,
y por un demonio un ángel?

TURÍN   Digo que razón te sobra:
que no está el gusto en el oro;
que son el oro y las horas   1060
muy diversas.

LISEO   Desde aquí
renuncio la dama boba.

Fin del primer acto de *La dama boba*

Act Two

Acto Segundo

ACTO SEGUNDO

ESCENA I

[Sala que da a un parque, en casa de Otavio.]
[Duardo, Laurencio, Feniso]

FENISO	En fin, ha pasado un mes	
	y no se casa Liseo.	
DUARDO	No siempre mueve el deseo	
	el codicioso interés.	
LAURENCIO	De Nise la enfermedad	
	ha sido causa bastante.	
FENISO	Ver a Finea ignorante	
	templará su voluntad.	1070
LAURENCIO	Menos lo está que solía.	
	Temo que amor ha de ser	
	artificioso a encender	
	piedra tan helada y fría.	
DUARDO	¡Tales milagros ha hecho	
	en gente rústica amor!	
FENISO	No se tendrá por menor	
	dar alma a su rudo pecho.	
LAURENCIO	Amor, señores, ha sido	
	aquel ingenio profundo,	1080
	que llaman alma del mundo,	
	y es el dotor que ha tenido	
	la cátedra de las ciencias;	
	porque sólo con amor	
	aprende el hombre mejor	
	sus divinas diferencias.	
	Así lo sintió Platón;	
	esto Aristóteles dijo;	
	que, como del cielo es hijo,	
	es todo contemplación.	1090
	De ella nació el admirarse,	
	y de admirarse nació	
	el filosofar, que dio	
	luz con que pudo fundarse	
	toda ciencia artificial.	

# Act Two

Scene 1

[Octavio's house—room facing a park.]
[Duardo, Laurencio, and Feniso]

FENISO   It's been a whole month and Liseo is still a bachelor!

DUARDO   Desire does not always breed greed.

LAURENCIO   Nise's illness is reason enough for the delay.

FENISO   Finding Finea so stupid cooled his passion, no doubt.

LAURENCIO   But she seems to be improving! However, love has to be artful if it's to set fire to that green log of a woman!

DUARDO   Love has worked miracles before.

FENISO   We won't think the less of it, if it plants a soul in her stony nature.

LAURENCIO   Love, gentlemen, is nothing less than that ingenious spirit, the soul of the world. It's a doctor who has held a chair in each of the sciences, for love alone can teach man the divine distinctions that make the sciences unique. Those, at least, were Plato's sentiments. And Aristotle claimed that, since it was born of heaven, love was all contemplation—giving birth to introspection; and from this contemplation of self, which lights the way for all the sciences, philosophy was born. We're indebted to Love then for man's thirst for knowledge. Love teaches man with gentle force to think and feel; it's given him laws for living soberly, honestly, wisely. Love has created republics, since concord was born of love—concord that heals the ravages of war. Love gave song to the birds, adorned the earth with fruits; and, as though it were a dry field in springtime, it plowed the sea with sturdy ships. By cause and effect, love has taught us to write sweet, elevated conceits; just as it has taught the coarsest,

Y a amor se ha de agradecer
que el deseo de saber
es al hombre natural.
    Amor con fuerza süave
dio al hombre el saber sentir,   1100
dio leyes para vivir,
político, honesto y grave.
    Amor repúblicas hizo;
que la concordia nació
de amor, con que a ser volvió
lo que la guerra deshizo.
    Amor dio lengua a las aves,
vistió la tierra de frutos,
y, como prados enjutos,
rompió el mar con fuertes naves.   1110
    Amor enseñó a escribir
altos y dulces concetos,
como de su causa efetos.
Amor enseñó a vestir
    al más rudo, al más grosero;
de la elegancia fue amor
el maestro; el inventor
fue de los versos primero;
    la música se le debe
y la pintura. Pues, ¿quién   1120
dejará de saber bien,
como sus efetos pruebe?
    No dudo de que a Finea,
como ella comience a amar,
la deje amor de enseñar,
por imposible que sea.

FENISO   Está bien pensado ansí,
y su padre lleva intento,
por dicha, en el casamiento,
que ame y sepa.   1130

DUARDO   Y yo de aquí,
infamando amores locos,
en limpio vengo a sacar
que pocos deben de amar
en lugar que saben pocos.

FENISO   ¡Linda malicia!

LAURENCIO   ¡Extremada!

FENISO   ¡Difícil cosa es saber!

LAURENCIO   Sí; pero fácil creer
que sabe, el que poco o nada.

rudest person to dress well, since elegance is its object. Love was the inventor of verse, and we are in its debt for music and painting. Well, then, who could remain ignorant that tastes love's fruit? I have no doubt, once she begins to love, love will transform Finea, impossible though it may seem.

FENISO   Well said! And her father has the same hopes in marrying her off, that she may love and learn!

DUARDO   But I proclaim, deriding ludicrous love affairs, that none should love where naught is known.

FENISO   Oh, well said!

LAURENCIO   Very!

FENISO   Knowledge is not easy to come by.

LAURENCIO   Yes! But it's easy for those who know nothing to assume they know it all.

FENISO   Nise's intelligence, on the other hand, is marvelous!

DUARDO   Celestial!

FENISO   How can illness, such a troublesome bore, dare attack so rare a genius as Nise!

LAURENCIO   The wise fall ill from suffering bores, or so they say.

DUARDO   She approaches.

FENISO   To gladden the hearts of all who behold her!

Scene II

[Enter Nise and Celia.]

NISE   *[To Celia]* I'm amazed!

CELIA   A passion, I'd say, founded upon money!

NISE   Love never built upon money; it prefers the soul.

FENISO	¡Qué divino entendimiento
	tiene Nise!
DUARDO	¡Celestial! 1140
FENISO	¿Cómo, siendo necio el mal,
	ha tenido atrevimiento
	para hacerle estos agravios,
	de tal ingenio desprecios?
LAURENCIO	Porque de sufrir a necios
	suelen enfermar los sabios.
DUARDO	Ella viene.
FENISO	Y con razón
	se alegra cuanto la mira.

ESCENA II

[Salen Nise, Celia.—Dichos]

NISE	*[Aparte a Celia]*
	Mucho la historia me admira.
CELIA	Amores pienso que son, 1150
	fundados en el dinero.
NISE	Nunca fundó su valor
	sobre dineros amor,
	que busca el alma primero.
DUARDO	Señora, a vuestra salud,
	hoy cuantas cosas os ven
	dan alegre parabién
	y tienen vida y quietud;
	que como vuestra virtud
	era el sol que se la dio, 1160
	mientras el mal le eclipsó
	también lo estuvieron ellas;
	que hasta ver vuestras estrellas
	Fortuna el tiempo corrió.
	Mas como la primavera
	sale con pies de marfil,
	y el vario velo sutil
	tiende en la verde ribera,
	corre el agua lisonjera
	y están riñendo las flores 1170
	sobre tomar las colores,
	así vos salís, trocando
	el triste tiempo y sembrando
	en campos de almas amores.
FENISO	Ya se ríen estas fuentes,
	y son perlas las que fueron

DUARDO M'lady, what ere beholds you today greets your health with a
happy welcome and enjoys peace and good life; for, since your
virtue was the sun that granted them existence, they were
eclipsed by your illness. Without your light the sky stormed
o'er. But—as when springtime emerges on its ivory feet, spread-
ing its variegated veil upon the grassy banks, the streams babble
flirtatiously, and flowers fight among themselves for her col-
ors—so you emerge, dispelling a sorry time, sowing love in the
fields of the soul!

FENISO These fountains begin to smile that wept tears, now pearls, for
the absence of those limpid stars, your eyes; the plashing
waters of the fountains prompt the birds to chirping with clear
and musical sound to celebrate your return. All things pine to
behold you and strive to offer you their most pleasing aspect.
Thus, if but the sight of you can cause such effects in things
that have no soul, m'lady—no more than that which you have
granted me—what wonders will you work, what signs of joy
upon this blessed day, and after so many disappointments, on
my seeing you, you who are the light of my eyes, the soul of
my soul!

LAURENCIO Unable to court you, I gave up living, and of the two things, I
missed most being able to court you. As a body that takes its
life from you, I languished with you. You had given me strength
with which to live, I am your instrument. My life, my health are
reflections of your own.Then greet me with good wishes with
the health that you enjoy. We suffered illness together! I
wronged you only in that—and I proffer my excuse—the illness
which was jointly ours, should not have been suffered alone by
you, but by me whose body is your slave, for you are my soul
entire!

NISE It would appear that you wish me well as an excuse to vie with
one another.

LAURENCIO Justly so, since we live for you and are your servants.

NISE Be kind, you two, and gather me some flowers from the garden.
Their precious variety invites you! I want to talk to Laurencio
for a while.

lágrimas, con que sintieron
esas estrellas ausentes;
y a las aves sus corrientes
hacen instrumentos claros   1180
con que quieren celebraros.
Todo se anticipa a veros,
y todo intenta ofreceros
con lo que puede alegraros.
    Pues si con veros hacéis
tales efetos agora,
donde no hay alma, señora,
más de la que vos ponéis,
en mí, ¿qué muestras haréis,
qué señales de alegría,   1190
este venturoso día,
después de tantos enojos,
siendo vos sol de mis ojos,
siendo vos alma en la mía?

LAURENCIO   A estar sin vida llegué
el tiempo que no os serví;
que fue lo más que sentí,
aunque sin mi culpa fue.
Yo vuestros males pasé,
como cuerpo que animáis;   1200
vos movimiento me dais,
yo soy instrumento vuestro,
que en mi vida y salud muestro
todo lo que vos pasáis.
    Parabién me den a mí
de la salud que hay en vos,
pues que pasamos los dos
el mismo mal en que os vi.
Solamente os ofendí,
aunque la disculpa os muestro,   1210
en que este mal que fue nuestro,
sólo tenerle debía,
no vos, que sois alma mía,
yo sí, que soy cuerpo vuestro.

NISE   Pienso que de oposición
me dais los tres parabién.

LAURENCIO Y es bien, pues lo sois por quien
viven los que vuestros son.

NISE   Divertíos, por mi vida,
cortándome algunas flores   1220
los dos, pues con sus colores
la diferencia os convida

DUARDO   He who loves in vain is either a madman or a fool!

FENISO   I expect no better fate!

DUARDO   My misgivings were justified!

FENISO   She loves *him*!

DUARDO   I'll make her a nosegay of devotion, but I'll trim it with jealousy.

[Feniso and Duardo leave.]

SCENE III

LAURENCIO   They've gone. May I, Nise, welcome back your health with my
            arms?

NISE   One side! You feigning, facile, fickle deceiver! You mad, incon-
            stant, mutable man, who, but in a single month of absence—for
            illness might well be called absence—have altered your affec-
            tion. But I should never have said a month! Because then you
            could claim that you thought I was dead, and, believing me
            dead, settled the accounts of my love with ever so tender senti-
            ment—before proceeding to transfer your own affection to
            Finea!

LAURENCIO   What are you saying?

NISE   Never fear, you're doing well. You're poor but cultured, she's
            rich but ignorant. You seek what you lack and reject what you
            have. You already possess intelligence and, therefore, with good
            reason, reject it in me, where once you praised it. Talents of
            equal measure are not apt to give in to one another. What! Do
            you imagine, by any chance, that I want that mastery which is
            generally conceded to men?! You sought the gold you lacked
            when you wooed Finea.

LAURENCIO   Hear me!

NISE   What could you possibly say for yourself?

| | de este jardín, porque quiero | |
| | hablar a Laurencio un poco. | |

DUARDO   Quien ama y sufre, o es loco
o necio.

FENISO   Tal premio espero.

DUARDO   No son vanos mis recelos.

FENISO   Ella le quiere.

DUARDO   Yo haré
un ramillete de fe,
pero sembrado de celos.   1230

[Vanse Duardo y Feniso.]

ESCENA III

LAURENCIO   Ya se han ido. ¿Podré yo,
Nise, con mis brazos darte
parabién de tu salud?

NISE   ¡Desvía, fingido, fácil,
lisonjero, engañador,
loco, inconstante, mudable
hombre, que en un mes de ausencia
—que bien merece llamarse
ausencia la enfermedad—,
el pensamiento mudaste!   1240
Pero mal dije en un mes,
porque puedes disculparte
con que creíste mi muerte,
y, si mi muerte pensaste,
con gracioso sentimiento,
pagaste el amor que sabes,
mudando el tuyo en Finea.

LAURENCIO   ¿Qué dices?

NISE   Pero bien haces:
tú eres pobre, tú discreto,
ella rica y ignorante;   1250
buscaste lo que no tienes,
y lo que tienes dejaste.
Discreción tienes, y en mí
la que celebrabas antes
dejas con mucha razón;
que dos ingenios iguales
no conocen superior;
y, por dicha, ¿imaginaste
que quisiera yo el imperio
que a los hombres debe darse?   1260

LAURENCIO   Who could have accused me of being so inconstant, and within a month?

NISE   Does it seem so short a time? Say no more. I forgive you. The moon in the sky, without human motives, in one month—nay less—grows full and wanes. But for you—here on earth, in Madrid, whipped about by so many stormy motives, it's no miracle, your waning. Celia, tell him what you saw!

CELIA   Don't be surprised, Laurencio, that my lady Nise treats you in this fashion. I know that you've been courting Finea!

LAURENCIO   Lies! How could you invent such things?

CELIA   You know it's true. And you weren't the only one ungrateful to my mistress! Your Pedro, who holds the key to your secrets, is now tenderly in pursuit of Clara. Shall I continue to testify?

LAURENCIO   Celia, you're jealous and want me to pay the bill! What? Pedro and Clara! That booby!

NISE   If you taught him, why take offense at that which your blindness hides from you? You remind me of an astrologer forever forecasting the bad luck of others and ignoring your own. How well you employ your wit! "I admire Nise's figure, yet beauty is but a shell!" Oh! To hear the two of you talking! Conversing in couplets of fractured rhyme! For welding a wise man to a fool is nothing short of poetic crime! Oh, Laurencio, how you repay an honest love! How right they are who claim that friends are tested in sickness and jail! I grew sick from sorrow, not seeing you and talking to you! They bled me—many times—and, oh, how you quickened my blood! What lovely presents you've made me: deceptions, betrayals, frauds! But they were all such hard presents I'm sure you would claim you gave me diamonds! Ah . . . enough of that!

LAURENCIO   Listen! Wait!

NISE   On you? Go woo your golden nitwit! Although I'll see that she's married sooner than you think.

LAURENCIO   Lady . . .

	El oro que no tenías,	
	tenerle solicitaste	
	enamorando a Finea.	
LAURENCIO	Escucha . . .	
NISE	¿Qué he de escucharte?	
LAURENCIO	¿Quién te ha dicho que yo he sido	
	en un mes tan inconstante?	

NISE
¿Parécete poco un mes?
Yo te disculpo, no hables;
que la Luna está en el cielo
sin intereses mortales,   1270
y en un mes, y aun algo menos,
está creciente y menguante.
Tú en la tierra, y de Madrid,
donde hay tantos vendavales
de intereses en los hombres,
no fue milagro mudarte.
Dile, Celia, lo que has visto.

CELIA
Ya, Laurencio, no te espantes
de que Nise, mi señora,
de esta manera te trate: 1280
yo sé que has dicho a Finea
requiebros . . .

LAURENCIO
                        ¡Que me levantes,
Celia, tales testimonios! . . .

CELIA
Tú sabes que son verdades;
y no sólo tú a mi dueño
ingratamente pagaste,
pero tu Pedro, el que tiene
de tus secretos las llaves,
ama a Clara tiernamente.
¿Quieres que más te declare?   1290

LAURENCIO
Tus celos han sido, Celia,
y quieres que yo los pague.
¿Pedro a Clara, aquella boba?

NISE
Laurencio, si le enseñaste,
¿por qué te afrentas de aquello
en que de ciego no caes?
Astrólogo me pareces,
que siempre de ajenos males,
sin reparar en los suyos,
largos pronósticos hacen.   1300
¡Qué bien empleas tu ingenio!
«De Nise confieso el talle,
mas no es sólo el exterior

SCENE IV

[Enter Liseo overhearing Laurencio and Nise.]

LISEO   *[Aside]* Afraid my love would be discovered, my love now makes me the discoverer!

NISE   Let go!

LAURENCIO I don't want to.

LISEO   What have we here?

NISE   Laurencio was asking me to tear up some verses by an ignorant lady of his acquaintance. I refused.

LAURENCIO Perhaps you can persuade her. Why don't you ask her?

LISEO   If I have power anything to entreat, then, for the sake of my petitions, tar out what you know best.

NISE   Oh! Leave me, the two of you!   *[Nise and Celia leave.]*

SCENE V

LAURENCIO What a temper!

LISEO   I'm amazed that Nise deals with you so sharply.

LAURENCIO Put your mind to rest, Liseo. To be not "affable" is a defect of the wise.

LISEO   Have you anything to do?

LAURENCIO At your disposal.

LISEO   Well, we shall meet at the upper Prado this afternoon.

LAURENCIO Let's go. Wherever you say.

LISEO   Behind the Recoletos Convent. I'll speak to you there.

LAURENCIO If you mean to talk with a tongue of steel—though I hate the thought—I will leave my horse and attendants behind.

el que obliga a los que saben.»
¡Oh, quién os oyera juntos! . . .
Debéis de hablar en romances,
porque un discreto y un necio
no pueden ser consonantes.
¡Ay Laurencio, qué buen pago
de fe y amor tan notable!   1310
Bien dicen que a los amigos,
prueba la cama y la cárcel.
Yo enfermé de mis tristezas,
y, de no verte ni hablarte,
sangráronme muchas veces.
¡Bien me alegraste la sangre!
Por regalos tuyos tuve
mundazas, traiciones, fraudes;
pero, pues tan duros fueron,
di que me diste diamantes.   1320
Ahora bien: ¡esto cesó!

LAURENCIO ¡Oye aguarda! . . .

NISE   ¿Que te aguarde?
Pretende tu rica boba,
aunque yo haré que se case
más presto que tú lo piensas.

LAURENCIO ¡Señora! . . .

ESCENA IV

[Entre Liseo, y asga Laurencio a Nise.—Dichos]

LISEO   *[Aparte]*   Esperaba tarde
los desengaños; mas ya
no quiere amor que me engañe.

NISE   ¡Suelta!

LAURENCIO   ¡No quiero!

LISEO   ¿Qué es esto?

NISE   Dice Laurencio que rasgue   1330
unos versos que me dio
de cierta dama ignorante,
y yo digo que no quiero.

LAURENCIO Tú podrá ser que lo alcances
de Nise; ruégalo tú.

LISEO   Si algo tengo que rogarte,
haz algo por mis memorias
y rasga lo que tú sabes.

NISE   ¡Dejadme los dos!   *[Vanse Nise y Celia.]*

LISEO   Well you might.   *[Liseo leaves.]*

SCENE VI

LAURENCIO   I'll follow you. How jealous and headstrong! It's all because Finea is a nitwit and has told him of my love, shown him my letters. Well, it's too late to remedy. Debts and challenges, if they're put off, snare the honesty of a man. It's best to settle them with dispatch!   *[Laurencio leaves.]*

SCENE VII

[Dancing Master enters with Finea.]

MASTER   Tired so soon?

FINEA   Yes! And I don't want to dance any more!

MASTER   You're angry because you cannot keep time!

FINEA   You bet I am angry! I almost fell on my face with all that hopping. Do you think I'm a magpie to go hippity-hoppiting around the house? One-step, counterstep, here-a-turn, there-a-turn, everywhere-you . . . What madness!

MASTER   *[Aside]* How could nature pour the liquor of such an imperfect soul into such a lovely vial?! She, once and for all, settles the question of whether beauty lies in body or soul!

FINEA   Master.

MASTER   M'lady.

FINEA   Bring a tambourine tomorrow.

MASTER   That's such a vulgar instrument! Although I grant you, it's a lively one.

FINEA   I'm also very fond of jingle bells!

ESCENA V

LAURENCIO	¡Qué airada!
LISEO	Yo me espanto que te trate 1340 con estos rigores Nise.
LAURENCIO	Pues, Liseo, no te espantes: que es defeto en los discretos tal vez el no ser afables.
LISEO	¿Tienes qué hacer?
LAURENCIO	Poco o nada.
LISEO	Pues vámonos esta tarde por el Prado arriba.
LAURENCIO	Vamos donde quiera que tú mandes.
LISEO	Detrás de los Recoletos quiero hablarte.
LAURENCIO	Si el hablarme 1350 no es con las lenguas que dicen, sino con lenguas que hacen, aunque me espanto que sea, dejaré caballo y pajes.
LISEO	Bien puedes. *[Vase.]*

ESCENA VI

[Laurencio solo]

LAURENCIO	Yo voy tras ti. ¡Qué celoso y qué arrogante! Finea es boba, y, sin duda, de haberle contado nace mis amores y papeles. Ya para consejo es tarde; 1360 que deudas y desafíos a que honrados salen, para trampas se dilatan, y no es bien que se dilaten. *[Vase.]*

ESCENA VII

[Un maestro de danzar y Finea]

MAESTRO	¿Tan presto se cansa?
FINEA	Sí. Y no quiero danzar más.

MASTER	They're better suited to horses!
FINEA	Do as I say! It's not vulgar to dance with bells on one's feet. It's much worse to have bells in your batfry!
MASTER	[Aside] I'll humor her. M'lady, as you please.
FINEA	Good. Now dance your way out of here!
MASTER	You flatter me, but I'll make a spectacle of myself!
FINEA	So what? Don't bakers, tailors, and cobblers draw crowds on the street to see their wares?
MASTER	Yes, but they don't ply their trade on the sidewalk!
FINEA	They could if they wanted.
MASTER	They might but I won't! I will not dance!
FINEA	Then don't bother to come back!
MASTER	I won't! Never again!
FINEA	Then don't!
MASTER	I won't!
FINEA	And I don't intend to spend my days balancing on one foot, spinning in the air, and bouncing up and down!
MASTER	Nor will I teach a lunatic possessed by such mad fancies!
FINEA	It's no skin off my nose! Husbands are the best teachers!
MASTER	Has there ever been such a nincompoop!
FINEA	Nincompoop—what?
MASTER	Hold, good lady, your hand! The word, m'lady, signifies one who treats her servants sternly and severely.
FINEA	Ha?
MASTER	Provided, of course, she relents and treats them with love and kindness.
FINEA	Is that true?

MAESTRO   Como no danza a compás,
           hase enfadado de sí.

FINEA   ¡Por poco diera de hocicos,
           saltando! Enfadada vengo.   1370
           ¿Soy yo urraca, que andar tengo
           por casa, dando salticos?
               Un paso, otro contrapaso,
           floretas, otra floreta . . .
           ¡Qué locura!

MAESTRO   *[Aparte]*   Qué imperfeta
           cosa, en un hermoso vaso
               poner la Naturaleza
           licor de un alma tan ruda!
           Con que yo salgo de duda
           que no es alma la belleza.   1380

FINEA   Maestro . . .

MAESTRO   ¿Señora mía? . . .

FINEA   Trae mañana un tamboril.

MAESTRO   Ése es instrumento vil,
           aunque de mucha alegría.

FINEA   Que soy más aficionada
           al cascabel os confieso.

MAESTRO   Es muy de caballos eso.

FINEA   Haced vos lo que me agrada,
               que no es mucha rustiqueza
           el traellos en los pies.   1390
           Harto peor pienso que es
           traellos en la cabeza.

MAESTRO   *[Aparte]*
               (Quiero seguirle el humor.)
           Yo haré lo que me mandáis.

FINEA   Id denzando cuando os vais.

MAESTRO   Yo os agradezco el favor,
               pero llevaré tras mí
           mucha gente.

FINEA   Un pastelero,
           un sastre y un zapatero,
           ¿llevan la gente tras sí?   1400

MAESTRO   No; pero tampoco ellos
           por la calle haciendo van
           sus oficios.

FINEA   ¿No podrán,
           si quieren?

MASTER	Of course.
FINEA	Then I swear there was never in the whole world a greater nincompoop than I!
MASTER	Credulity is tantamount to courtesy. And at this juncture, madam, you are all courtesy! Good-bye.

[He leaves. Clara enters.]

SCENE VIII

CLARA	Through dancing?
FINEA	Can't you tell? They hound me all day long to read, write, and dance, and it's all for nothing! Laurencio is the only thing that pleases me!
CLARA	How can I give you the terrible news?
FINEA	By talking. If a woman is alive and can talk, there's nothing she won't lay her tongue to.
CLARA	Is it bad to sleep late on a feast day?
FINEA	I don't think so; though oversleeping cost Adam his rib.
CLARA	Well, then, if woman was born of a sleeping rib, it's no wonder she likes to lie abed.
FINEA	With no more than your clue, I begin to understand why men are always pursuing us—courting one, then another! For, provided they aren't cribbing, they must be—ribbing! And there's no stopping them 'til they find their lost rib.
CLARA	And so it is with those who love a year or more, their friends may well assume they've found their lost rib.
FINEA	Provided, of course, they're married We have no ribs to spare.
CLARA	You're catching on.
FINEA	Taught by the cares of love. I am learning.

MAESTRO	Podrán hacellos;
	y yo no quiero danzar.
FINEA	Pues no entréis aquí.
MAESTRO	No haré.
FINEA	Ni quiero andar en un pie,
	ni dar vueltas ni saltar.
MAESTRO	Ni yo enseñar las que sueñan
	disparates atrevidos.
FINEA	No importa; que los maridos
	son los que mejor enseñan.
MAESTRO	¿Han visto la mentecata?
FINEA	¿Qué es mentecata, villano?
MAESTRO	¡Señora, tened la mano!
	Es una dama que trata
	con gravedad y rigor
	a quien la sirve.
FINEA	¿Ésa es?
MAESTRO	Puesto que vuelve después
	con más blandura y amor.
FINEA	¿Es eso cierto?
MAESTRO	¿Pues no?
FINEA	Yo os juro, aunque nunca ingrata,
	que no hay mayor mentecata
	en todo el mundo que yo.
MAESTRO.	El creer es cortesía;
	adiós, que soy muy cortés.

1410

1420

[Váyase y entre Clara.]

ESCENA VIII

CLARA	¿Danzaste?
FINEA	¿Ya no lo ves?
	Persíguenme todo el día
	con leer, con escribir,
	con danzar, y todo es nada.
	Sólo Laurencio me agrada.
CLARA	¿Cómo te podré decir
	una desgracia notable?
FINEA	Hablando; porque no hay cosa
	de decir dificultosa,
	a mujer que viva y hable.

1430

CLARA   But to the point. Laurencio gave me a note for you. I was spin-
         ning at the time. Oh, the way silence works on one! I stuck the
         paper on the distaff, and since I was spinning by the candle
         and the flax was so fine, the distaff caught fire. Forgive my
         nodding off! Last night I slept without a pillow and had more
         bad dreams than there are billows on the sea! The minute the
         distaff caught fire, I jumped up and stomped it out! I burned
         myself, see?

FINEA   And the note?

CLARA   Almost untouched, like Moses and the burning bush. You'll
         find more sentences in the lines that are left than I have hairs
         on my head.

FINEA   Can you make them out?

CLARA   Here—read them.

FINEA   I don't know how to read—well.

CLARA   God keep a mad flame from nesting in a woman's hemp.

SCENE IX

[Octavio enters.]

OCTAVIO I'm weary of trying to educate her; it's like carving marble with
         a piece of glass. She can neither learn to read nor dance,
         although she does seem less ignorant of late.

FINEA   Generous and most nincompoop Father, welcome!

OCTAVIO Nincompoop? What?

FINEA   My dancing master called me nincompoop and I got very angry
         with him, but he explained it meant a person who loses her
         temper and then repents. Now, since you come in anger and are
         soon to repent and show me love, I thought it only right to call
         you nincompoop.

CLARA   Dormir en día de fiesta,
               ¿es malo?

FINEA   Pienso que no;
               aunque si Adán se durmió,
               buena costilla le cuesta.   1440

CLARA   Pues si nació la mujer
               de una dormida costilla,
               que duerma no es maravilla.

FINEA   Agora vengo a entender
                   sólo con esa advertencia,
               por qué se andan tras nosotras
               los hombres, y en unas y otras
               hacen tanta diligencia;
                   que, si aquesto no es asilla,
               deben de andar a buscar   1450
               su costilla, y no hay parar
               hasta topar su costilla.

CLARA   Luego si para el que amó
               un año, y dos, harto bien,
               ¿le dirán los que le ven
               que su costilla topó?

FINEA   A lo menos los casados.

CLARA   ¡Sabia estás!

FINEA   Aprendo ya;
               que me enseña amor quizá
               con liciones de cuidados.   1460

CLARA   Volviendo al cuento, Laurencio
               me dio un papel para ti.
               Púseme a hilar —¡ay de mí,
               cuánto provoca el silencio!—.
                   Metí en el copo el papel,
               y como hilaba al candil
               y es la estopa tan sutil
               aprendióse el copo en él.
                   Cabezas hay disculpadas
               cuando duermen sin cojines,   1470
               y sueños como rocines
               que vienen con cabezadas.
                   Apenas el copo ardió,
               cuando, puesta en él de pies,
               me chamusqué; ya lo ves.

FINEA   ¿Y el papel?

CLARA   Libre quedó,
               como el Santo de Pajares.

OCTAVIO   Well, child, don't believe all you hear! And don't call me that again! It's not proper.

FINEA   I shan't. But tell me, Father, can you read?

OCTAVIO   What a question! Of course!

FINEA   Then, read this for me, please.

OCTAVIO   This paper?

FINEA   Yes, Father.

OCTAVIO   Very well. *[He reads.]* "I thank you for the favors you have shown me, even though they kept me awake all night thinking of your beauty."

FINEA   Is that all?

OCTAVIO   The rest of it is neatly burned away. Who sent you this?

FINEA   Laurencio, that wise gentleman from my sister Nise's academy. He claims he loves me very much.

OCTAVIO   *[Aside]* I'll be dishonored by her ignorance, I know it! And as for Nise, her learning has brought to this household nothing but lovers, musicians, poets, and fops—all stinking of perfume, beardless, mad, and lazy to boot! *[To Finea]* Has anything else passed between you two?

FINEA   On the stairway, yesterday, on the first landing, he gave me a hug.

OCTAVIO   *[Aside]* And what landings will my honor make, on one side or the other? The wise one cruises with idiots on a sea of conceits while the nitwit sails into love with a trickster! There's no point in punishing this one, Liseo might get wind of it! Daughter, know that I'm displeased. Do not allow yourself to be embraced! Do you understand me?

FINEA   Yes, Father. I'm sorry, although at the time it seemed quite nice.

OCTAVIO   Save your embraces for your husband.

	Sobraron estos renglones,	
	en que hallarás más razones	
	que en mi cabeza aladares.	1480

FINEA   ¿Y no se podrán leer?

CLARA   Toma, y lee.

FINEA   Yo sé poco.

CLARA   ¡Dios libre de un fuego loco
        la estopa de la mujer!

Escena IX

[Entre Otavio.—Dichas]

OTAVIO   Yo pienso que me canso en enseñarla,
        porque es querer labrar con vidro un pórfido;
        ni el danzar ni el leer aprender puede,
        aunque está menos ruda que solía.

FINEA   ¡Oh padre mentecato y generoso,
        bien seas venido!

OTAVIO   ¿Cómo mentecato?   1490

FINEA   Aquí el maestro de danzar me dijo
        que era yo mentecata, y enojéme;
        mas él me respondió que este vocablo
        significaba una mujer que riñe,
        y luego vuelve con amor notable;
        y como vienes tú riñendo agora,
        y has de mostrarme amor en breve rato,
        quise también llamarte mentecato.

OTAVIO   Pues, hija, no creáis a todas gentes,
        ni digáis ese nombre, que no es justo.   1500

FINEA   No lo haré más. Mas diga, señor padre:
        ¿sabe leer?

OTAVIO   Pues, ¿eso me preguntas?

FINEA   Tome, ¡por vida suya!, y éste lea.

OTAVIO   ¿Este papel?

FINEA   Sí, padre.

OTAVIO   Oye, Finea:
        [Lea ansí.]
        «Agradezco mucho la merced que me has hecho,
        aunque toda esta noche la he pasado con poco
        sosiego, pensando en tu hermosura.»

FINEA   ¿No hay más?

OTAVIO   No hay más; que está muy justamente
        quemado lo demás. ¿Quién te le ha dado?

SCENE X

[Enter Turín.]

TURÍN   I've been searching for you.

OCTAVIO   You're panting!

TURÍN   They've gone to the Prado to kill themselves—my master and
             Laurencio, that patchwork nobleman who dizzies Nise with his
             sonnets!

OCTAVIO   What earthly good is it for parents to be careful if their children
             are reckless? Liseo must have discovered that this mad, fool-
             hardy Laurencio has had the impertinence to court his bride!
             What a muddle! Where have they gone?

TURÍN   If I'm not mistaken, they're headed toward the Augustinian
             Recoletos.

OCTAVIO   Madness! Follow me!

[Octavio and Turín leave.]

SCENE XI

CLARA   Your father's angry.

FINEA   What can I do?

CLARA   Why did you give him the note?

FINEA   I've already regretted it.

CLARA   Now you'll have to give up Laurencio.

FINEA   That's asking me to give up my life! I don't know how, but
             from the moment he talked to me he robbed me of my senses.
             When I sleep, I dream of him; while I eat, I think of him; and
             when I drink, I see his image in the water. Have you ever
             noticed how a little self-deception turns your image in a mirror
             into solid flesh and blood? Well, it's like that with my images
             of him!

FINEA	Laurencio, aquel discreto caballero
	de la academia de mi hermana Nise,
	que dice que me quiere con extremo.

OTAVIO	*[Aparte]*
	(De su ignorancia, mi desdicha temo. 1510
	Esto trujo a mi casa el ser discreta
	Nise: El galán, el músico, el poeta,
	el lindo, el que se precia de oloroso,
	el afeitado, el loco y el ocioso.)
	¿Hate pasado más con éste, acaso?

| FINEA | Ayer, en la escalera, al primer paso, |
| | me dio un abrazo. |

OTAVIO	*[Aparte]* (¡En buenos pasos anda
	mi pobre honor, por una y otra banda!
	La discreta, con necios en concetos,
	y la boba, en amores con discretos. 1520
	A ésta no hay llevarla por castigo,
	y más que lo podrá entender su esposo.)
	Hija, sabed que estoy muy enojado.
	No os dejéis abrazar. ¿Entendéis, hija?

| FINEA | Sí, señor padre; y cierto que me pesa, |
| | aunque me pareció muy bien entonces. |

| OTAVIO | Sólo vuestro marido ha de ser digno |
| | de esos abrazos. |

ESCENA X

[Entre Turín.—Dichos]

| TURÍN | En tu busca vengo |

| OTAVIO | ¿De qué es la prisa tanta? |

TURÍN	De que al campo
	van a matarse mi señor Liseo 1530
	y Laurencio, ese hidalgo marquesote,
	que desvanece a Nise con sonetos.

OTAVIO	*[Aparte]*
	(¿Qué importa que los padres sean discretos,
	si les falta a los hijos la obediencia?
	Liseo habrá entendido la imprudencia
	deste Laurencio atrevidillo y loco,
	y que sirve a su esposa.) ¡Caso extraño!
	¿Por dónde fueron?

| TURÍN | Van, si no me engaño, |
| | hacia los Recoletos Agustinos. |

CLARA   I am amazed at the change in you! You're becoming another person!

FINEA   Because of another person.

CLARA   He's the best teacher you've had!

FINEA   In spite of that, I must obey my father. It would be monstrous if I broke my word.

CLARA   And I'll follow your example.

FINEA   Don't change because of me.

CLARA   Can't you understand? I loved because you loved and I'll forget because you forget!

FINEA   I'm going to miss not loving him, but I see the danger I'm in. Although I may just have to forget to forget him.

         [They leave.]

SCENE XII

[Countryside.]

[Liseo and Laurencio enter.]

LAURENCIO   Liseo, before you draw, tell me the cause that prompts you.

LISEO   That's only fair.

LAURENCIO   If it's jealousy of Finea, I have a right to court her until the banns are proclaimed. I declared myself first.

LISEO   As I am a gentleman, you dissemble! But I know how far your thoughts are from loving that nitwit!

LAURENCIO   That I want her shouldn't surprise you; I'm as poor as I am highborn and I want to support myself with the crutch of her dowry. I confess it! This should give you no cause for alarm, for in postponing your wedding you encouraged me in my intent. When it becomes necessary to undress one's sword in a duel,

OTAVIO   Pues ven tras mí. ¡Qué extraños desatinos!   1540

[Váyanse Otavio y Turín.]

ESCENA XI

CLARA   Parece que se ha enojado
            tu padre.

FINEA   ¿Qué puedo hacer?

CLARA   ¿Por qué le diste a leer
            el papel?

FINEA   Ya me ha pesado.

CLARA   Ya no puedes proseguir
            la voluntad de Laurencio.

FINEA   Clara, no la diferencio
            con el dejar de vivir.
                Yo no entiendo cómo ha sido
            desde que el hombre me habló,   1550
            porque, si es que siento yo,
            él me ha llevado el sentido.
                Si duermo, sueño con él;
            si como, le estoy pensando,
            y si bebo, estoy mirando
            en agua la imagen dél.
                ¿No has visto de qué manera
            muestra el espejo a quien mira
            su rostro, que una mentira
            le hace forma verdadera?   1560
                Pues lo mismo en vidro miro
            que el cristal me representa.

CLARA   A tus palabras atenta,
            de tus mudanzas me admiro.
                Parece que te transformas
            en otra.

FINEA   Y en otro dirás.

CLARA   Es maestro con quien más
            para aprender te conformas.

FINEA   Con todo eso, seré
            obediente al padre mío;   1570
            fuera de que es desvarío
            quebrar la palabra y fe.

CLARA   Yo haré lo mismo.

FINEA   No impidas
            el camino que llevabas.

one should also lay bare the truth. It's vile to tell lies on the field of honor.

LISEO   You're not in love with Nise?

LAURENCIO   I don't deny that I loved her once. But her dowry is fixed at ten thousand ducats, and between ten and forty there lie thirty thousand reasons to raise myself to forty.

LISEO   And I believe you. Rest assured, I'll not interfere with your designs upon Finea. Though she may not have the luck of an ugly woman, she certainly has that of an ignorant one! And may God grant her thus to me! From the moment I saw Nise I surrendered my life to her!

LAURENCIO   Nise?

LISEO   Yes.

LAURENCIO   She's yours! With the blessings of my elder love, I bestow on you all the hopes and favors I once enjoyed. I give you my desires, love, worries, insomnia, my vigils, verse, suspicions, and jealousies! But take my score of triumphs, double the stakes, and she still will hold your ace!

LISEO   Even though I were dealt marked cards, I'd accept your offer, Laurencio. I am rich enough to buy my pleasure. Nise is wise; what more could I want? I have gold aplenty so it's Nise I'll adore!

LAURENCIO   Well done. For my part, since I'm poor, I seek gold and some to spare! Though Finea is poor of intellect, I want her to be the jewel of my home. One may keep a property locked up in a desk, but may it not provide one with food to last the year long? And may not a house of stone or, at least brick and mortar, bring as much as a thousand ducats on a lease? Well, I'll make believe that Finea is such a house, such a deed, income, vineyard—a property in petticoats! Furthermore, it is enough that she love me. Woman has no greater virtue than fidelity.

LISEO   I'll help you; I give you my word. No one could wish her to be more yours than I!

CLARA   ¿No ves que amé porque amabas,
             y olvidaré porque olvidas?

FINEA   Harto me pesa de amalle;
             pero a ver mi daño vengo,
             aunque sospecho que tengo
             de olvidarme de olvidalle.   *[Váyanse.]*   1580

ESCENA XII

[Campo]

[Entren Liseo y Laurencio.]

LAURENCIO   Antes, Liseo, de sacar la espada,
             quiero saber la causa que os obliga.

LISEO   Pues bien será que la razón os diga.

LAURENCIO   Liseo, si son celos de Finea,
             mientras no sé que vuestra esposa sea,
             bien puedo pretender, pues fui primero.

LISEO   Disimuláis, a fe de caballero,
             pues tan lejos lleváis el pensamiento
             de amar una mujer tan inorante.

LAURENCIO   Antes de que la quiera no os espante;   1590
             que soy tan pobre como bien nacido,
             y quiero sustentarme con el dote.
             Y que lo diga ansí no os alborote,
             pues que vos, dilatando el casamiento,
             habéis dado más fuerzas a mi intento,
             y porque cuando llegan, obligadas,
             a desnudarse en campo las espadas,
             se han de tratar verdades llanamente;
             que es hombre vil quien en el campo miente.

LISEO   ¿Luego, no queréis bien a Nise?

LAURENCIO   A Nise   1600
             yo no puedo negar que no la quise;
             mas su dote serán diez mil ducados,
             y de cuarenta a diez, ya veis, van treinta,
             y pasé de los diez a los cuarenta.

LISEO   Siendo eso ansí, como de vos lo creo,
             estad seguro que jamás Liseo
             os quite la esperanza de Finea;
             que aunque no es la ventura de la fea,
             será de la ignorante la ventura;
             que así Dios me la dé, que no la quiero,   1610
             pues desde que la vi, por Nise muero.

LAURENCIO   ¿Por Nise?

LAURENCIO   And my endeavors to help you to Nise will be as evident, by
              God.

LISEO   Shake hands on it as friends—not shallow courtiers, but as
              Greeks who knew the value of friendship.

LAURENCIO   I shall be your Pylades.

LISEO   And I your Orestes.

Scene XIII

[Octavio and Turín enter.]

OCTAVIO   Are these the ones?

TURÍN   They are.

OCTAVIO   Is this what you call dueling?

TURÍN   They must have seen your approach.

OCTAVIO   Gentlemen . . .

LISEO   Welcome, sir.

OCTAVIO   What are you doing here?

LISEO   Laurencio has been so generous and friendly since I arrived at
              your house—or, rather, my home—that we have come to the
              Prado to talk over our affairs.

OCTAVIO   Your friendship pleases me. I was on my way to visit the gardens
              of a friend and I would be most pleased if you would join me.

LISEO   We're honored.

LAURENCIO   We'll accompany you and serve you. Lead on.

OCTAVIO   Turín, you deceived me! Why?!

TURÍN   They're pretending or else they have made their peace, which is
              the usual death of most quarrels—otherwise, there'd be no one
              left in Madrid!

LISEO	¡Sí, por Dios!
LAURENCIO	Pues vuestra es Nise,

y con la antigüedad que yo la quise,
yo os doy sus esperanzas y favores;
mis deseos os doy y mis amores,
mis ansias, mis serenos, mis desvelos,
mis versos, mis sospechas y mis celos.
Entrad con esta runfla y dalde pique;
que no hará mucho en que de vos se pique.

LISEO   Aunque con cartas tripuladas juegue,   1620
aceto la merced, señor Laurencio,
que yo soy rico, y compraré mi gusto.
Nise es discreta, yo no quiero el oro;
hacienda tengo, su belleza adoro.

LAURENCIO Hacéis muy bien; que yo, que soy tan pobre,
el oro solicito que me sobre;
que aunque de entendimiento lo es Finea,
yo quiero que en mi casa alhaja sea.
¿No están las escrituras de una renta
en un cajón de un escritorio, y rinden   1630
aquello que se come todo el año?
¿No está una casa principal tan firme
como de piedra, al fin yeso y ladrillo,
y renta mil ducados a su dueño?
Pues yo haré cuenta que es Finea una casa,
una escritura, un censo y una viña,
y seráme una renta con basquiña;
demás que, si me quiere, a mí me basta;
que no hay mayor ingenio que ser casta.

LISEO   Yo os doy palabra de ayudaros tanto,   1640
que venga a ser tan vuestra como creo.

LAURENCIO Y yo con Nise haré, por Dios, Liseo,
lo que veréis.

LISEO   Pues démonos las manos
de amigos, no fingidos cortesanos,
sino como si fuéramos de Grecia,
adonde tanto el amistad se precia.

LAURENCIO Yo seré vuestro Pílades.

LISEO   Yo, Orestes.

ESCENA XIII

[Entren Otavio y Turín.—Dichos]

OTAVIO   ¿Son éstos?

TURÍN   Ellos son.

OCTAVIO	Could they have settled their differences so quickly?
Turín	What better argument for peace than the price of one's life?

[They leave.]

SCENE XIV

[Room in Octavio's house.]

[Finea and Nise enter.]

NISE	You've become so conceited I no longer recognize you!
FINEA	You do me wrong; I've not changed.
NISE	I remember when you were . . . less canny!
FINEA	And I recall when you were more composed.
NISE	Who's changing you? Who's your secret tutor? Your mind's improved. You haven't been taking anacardium to improve your memory, have you?
FINEA	I have never taken classes from any Anna or Cardium either! I'm the same person I used to be. If I've changed it's because I'm more troubled than I used to be.
NISE	Laurencio is a jewel that belongs to me! You know that!
FINEA	Who pawned him with you?
NISE	Love pawned him!
FINEA	Did he? Well, then, I redeemed him, and love pawned him again with me!
NISE	I could kill you a thousand times over! Lucky idiot!
FINEA	Wanting Laurencio isn't going to make him yours. What little I've learned in my life, I've learned from him. And this I know, this I've learned!

OTAVIO	¿Y esto es pendencia?	
TURÍN	Conocieron de lejos tu presencia.	
OTAVIO	¡Caballeros . . . !	
LISEO	Señor, seáis bien venido.	1650
OTAVIO	¿Qué hacéis aquí?	

LISEO
                    Como Laurencio ha sido
tan grande amigo mío, desde el día
que vine a vuestra casa, o a la mía,
venímonos a ver el campo solos,
tratando nuestras cosas igualmente.

OTAVIO
De esa amistad me huelgo extrañamente.
Aquí vine a un jardín de un grande amigo,
y me holgaré de que volváis conmigo.

| LISEO | Será para los dos merced notable. | |
| LAURENCIO | Vamos [a] acompañaros y serviros. | 1660 |

OTAVIO
[Aparte]
Turín, ¿por qué razón me has engañado?

TURÍN
Porque deben de haber disimulado,
y porque, en fin, las más de las pendencias
mueren por madurar; que a no ser esto,
no hubiera mundo ya.

OTAVIO
                    Pues, di, ¿tan presto
se pudo remediar?

TURÍN
               ¿Qué más remedio
de no reñir que estar la vida en medio?   *[Vanse.]*

ESCENA XIV

[Sala en casa de Otavio.]

[Nise y Finea]

NISE
        De suerte te has engreído,
que te voy desconociendo.

FINEA
De que eso digas me ofendo.   1670
Yo soy la que siempre he sido.

NISE
        Yo te vi menos discreta.

FINEA
Y yo más segura a ti.

NISE
¿Quién te va trocando ansí?
¿Quién te da lición secreta?
        Otra memoria es la tuya.
¿Tomaste la anacardina?

FINEA
Ni de Ana, ni Catalina,
he tomado lición suya.
        Aquello que ser solía   1680

NISE	Clever aren't you?! But henceforth he's to cross your mind no more!
FINEA	Who?
NISE	Laurencio.
FINEA	You're right, and you'll have no cause for complaint.
NISE	If he sets his eyes on you don't let yours answer.
FINEA	As you wish.
NISE	Finea, leave Laurencio for me! You *have* a sweetheart.
FINEA	We have no quarrel.
NISE	God be with you.
FINEA	Good-bye.

SCENE XV

[Nise leaves and Laurencio enters.]

FINEA	Oh, what confusion! Is there a woman more wretched than I? They're all against me!
LAURENCIO	*[Aside]* Swift and fleeting fortune, halt! At last you appear to be on the brink of helping my cause. What a beautiful opportunity! Is that you, my love?
FINEA	Don't ever hope to see me again, Laurencio. All of them are quarreling with me because of you!
LAURENCIO	What reports have they made of me?
FINEA	You'll know soon enough. Oh, what am I thinking of? Where are my thoughts?
LAURENCIO	Your thoughts?
FINEA	Yes.

               soy; porque sólo he mudado
               un poco de más cuidado.

NISE   ¿No sabes que es prenda mía
               Laurencio?

FINEA   ¿Quién te empeñó
               a Laurencio?

NISE   Amor.

FINEA   ¿A fe?
               Pues yo le desempeñé,
               y el mismo amor me le dio.

NISE   ¡Quitaréte dos mil vidas,
               boba dichosa!

FINEA   No creas
               que si a Laurencio deseas,   1690
               de Laurencio te dividas.
                En mi vida supe más
               de lo que él me ha dicho a mí:
               eso sé y eso aprendí.

NISE   Muy aprovechada estás;
                mas de hoy más no ha de pasarte
               por el pensamiento.

FINEA   ¿Quién?

NISE   Laurencio.

FINEA   Dices muy bien.
               No volverás a quejarte.

NISE   Si los ojos puso en ti,   1700
               quítelos luego.

FINEA   Que sea
               como tú quieres.

NISE   Finea.
               déjame a Laurencio a mí.
                Marido tienes.

FINEA   Yo creo
               que no riñamos las dos.

NISE   Quédate con Dios.

FINEA   Adiós.   *[Váyase Nise.]*

ESCENA XV

[Entre Laurencio.—Finea]

FINEA   ¡En qué confusión me veo!
                ¿Hay mujer más desdichada?
               Todos dan en perseguirme.

LAURENCIO	In yourself, because if they were on me, I would be happier than I am.
FINEA	Can you see them?
LAURENCIO	No, never.
FINEA	My sister just told me that you were not to cross my mind. So turn around, and don't cross it again!
LAURENCIO	*[Aside]* She thinks I'm inside her mind and wants to expel me.
FINEA	And what's more, she says you set your eyes on me!
LAURENCIO	She's right! By my soul, I don't deny it.
FINEA	Well, pluck them off!
LAURENCIO	How can I and still love?
FINEA	Take them off me at once, I beg you! If they happen to be on my eyes—here, use my handkerchief.
LAURENCIO	Enough. Don't worry.
FINEA	They're not on my eyes?
LAURENCIO	Yes.
FINEA	Well, use the handkerchief and get rid of them because they're not supposed to be there.
LAURENCIO:	What charming fancies!
FINEA	Put them on Nise's eyes where they belong.
LAURENCIO	All right. With the handkerchief.
FINEA	Are they gone?
LAURENCIO	Can't you tell?
FINEA	Laurencio, don't give them to her; I take them back! Oh, but there's more! My father is furious about the hug you gave me!
LAURENCIO	*[Aside]* Another bumble!
FINEA	You must take that back too. I don't want to be scolded on that account either.

LAURENCIO   [Aparte]
            (Detente en un punto firme,   1710
            fortuna veloz y airada,
                que ya parece que quieres
            ayudar mi pretensión.
            ¡Oh, qué gallarda ocasión!)
            ¿Eres tú, mi bien?

FINEA   No esperes,
                Laurencio, verme jamás.
            Todos me riñen por ti.

LAURENCIO   Pues, ¿qué te han dicho de mí?

FINEA   Eso agora lo sabrás.
                ¿Dónde está mi pensamiento?   1720

LAURENCIO   ¿Tu pensamiento?

FINEA   Sí.

LAURENCIO   En ti;
            porque si estuviera en mí,
            ya estuviera más contento.

FINEA   ¿Vesle tú?

LAURENCIO   Yo no, jamás.

FINEA   Mi hermana me dijo aquí
            que no has de pasarme a mí
            por el pensamiento más;
                por eso allá te desvía,
            y no me pases por él.

LAURENCIO   [Aparte]
            Piensa que yo estoy en él,   1730
            y echarme fuera querría.

FINEA   Tras esto dice que en mí
            pusiste los ojos . . .

LAURENCIO   Dice
            verdad; no lo contradice
            el alma que vive en ti.

FINEA   Pues tú me has de quitar luego
            los ojos que me pusiste.

LAURENCIO   ¿Cómo, si en amor consiste?

FINEA   Que me los quites, te ruego,
                con ese lienzo, de aquí,   1740
            si yo los tengo en mis ojos.

LAURENCIO   No más; cesen los enojos.

FINEA   ¿No están en mis ojos?

LAURENCIO   Sí.

LAURENCIO But how can I do that?

FINEA   Well, you're quick-witted; don't you know how to un-hug?

LAURENCIO Now let me see. I raised my right arm. That's it! Now I remember! So now I'll raise my left arm and thus undo my embrace.

FINEA   Am I disembraced?

LAURENCIO Can't you tell?

SCENE XVI

[Nise enters.]

NISE   Well I can!

FINEA   I'm doing so well, Nise! You'll have no cause to scold me ever again! Laurencio isn't going to cross my mind any more. And since he's engaged to you, I gave him back his eyes! See, here! He's got them in the handkerchief! And he's just finished disembracing me!

LAURENCIO *[Aside, to Nise]* You'll have a good laugh when I tell you what's happened.

NISE   Not here! Let's go into the garden; there's more than enough for the two of us to quarrel over!

LAURENCIO Wherever you wish.

[Laurencio and Nise leave.]

SCENE XVII

FINEA   And so she just takes him away! Why am I disturbed when she goes off with him? I'm on the verge of running after him! I'm a stranger to my own will! Why? I am not myself without

FINEA   Pues limpia y quita los tuyos,
                 que no han de estar en los míos.

LAURENCIO   ¡Qué graciosos desvaríos!

FINEA   Ponlos a Nise en los suyos.

LAURENCIO   Ya te limpio con el lienzo.

FINEA   ¿Quitástelos?

LAURENCIO   ¿No lo ves?

FINEA   Laurencio, no se los des,   1750
                 que a sentir penas comienzo.
                     Pues más hay: que el padre mío
                 bravamente se ha enojado
                 del abrazo que me has dado.

LAURENCIO   *[Aparte]*
                 ¿Mas que hay otro desvarío?

FINEA   También me le has de quitar;
                 no ha de reñirme por esto.

LAURENCIO   ¿Cómo ha de ser?

FINEA   Siendo. Presto,
                 ¿no sabes desabrazar?

LAURENCIO   El brazo derecho alcé;   1760
                 tienes razón, ya me acuerdo,
                 y agora alzaré el izquierdo,
                 y el abrazo desharé.

FINEA   ¿Estoy ya desabrazada?

LAURENCIO   ¿No lo ves?

ESCENA XVI

[Entre Nise.—Dichos]

NISE   Y yo también.

FINEA   Huélgome, Nise, también,
                 que ya no me dirás nada.
                     Ya Laurencio no me pasa
                 por el pensamiento a mí;
                 ya los ojos le volví,   1770
                 pues que contigo se casa.
                     En el lienzo los llevó,
                 y ya me ha desabrazado.

LAURENCIO   Tú sabrás lo que ha pasado,
                 con harta risa.

Laurencio. Here's my father! Silence! Tongue, be still; and eyes, speak for me.

Scene XVIII

[Octavio enters.]

OCTAVIO   Where's Liseo?

FINEA   I thought the first thing you'd want to know is whether I'd obeyed you.

OCTAVIO   To what purpose?

FINEA   You told me I did wrong when I embraced Laurencio. Well, I asked him just now to disembrace me. The embrace is now dissolved!

OCTAVIO   Who ever heard such nonsense! Were you embracing him again, you booby?

FINEA   Certainly not. The first time Laurencio hugged me, he raised his right arm like this, and this time—I remember very well, because it was the other way around—this time he raised his left arm. So you see, I'm disembraced.

OCTAVIO   *[Aside]* Every time I think she's improving, she proves she knows less than ever! I suppose it's asking too much of nature for her to change.

FINEA   Father, what does one call the feeling that comes when the person one loves goes off with another?

OCTAVIO   That agony of love is called jealousy.

FINEA   Jealousy?

OCTAVIO   It's love's offspring.

FINEA   The father may bestow a thousand delights and be very kind; but how he must suffer, having reared such a bad child.

NISE   Aquí no.
                  Vamos los dos al jardín,
                  que tengo bien que riñamos.
LAURENCIO   Donde tú quisieras vamos.

                  [Váyanse Laurencio y Nise.]

ESCENA XVII

FINEA   Ella se le lleva, en fin.
                  ¿Qué es esto, que me da pena   1780
             de que se vaya con él?
             Estoy por irme tras él.
             ¿Qué es esto que me enajena
                  de mi propia libertad?
             No me hallo sin Laurencio.
             Mi padre es éste; silencio.
             Callad, lengua; ojos, hablad.

ESCENA XVIII

[Entre Otavio.—Finea]

OTAVIO   ¿Adónde está tu esposo?
FINEA   Yo pensaba
             que lo primero, en viéndome, que hicieras
             fuera saber de mí si te obedezco.   1790
OTAVIO   Pues eso, ¿a qué propósito?
FINEA   ¿Enojado
             no me dijiste aquí que era mal hecho
             abrazar a Laurencio? Pues agora
             que me desabrazase le he rogado,
             y el abrazo pasado me ha quitado.
OTAVIO   ¿Hay cosa semejante? ¡Pues di, bestia!,
             ¿otra vez le abrazabas?
FINEA   Que no es eso:
             fue la primera alzado el brazo
             derecho de Laurencio, aquél abrazo,
             y agora levantó, que bien me acuerdo,   1800
             porque fuese al revés, el brazo izquierdo:
             luego desabrazada estoy agora.
OTAVIO   *[Aparte]*
             Cuando pienso que sabe, más ignora;
             ello es querer hacer lo que no quiso
             Naturaleza.

OCTAVIO	*[Aside]* Do I begin to see a glimmer of light? Indeed, if love were to teach her, she might very well learn.
FINEA	How does one cure jealousy?
OCTAVIO	If there is cause, by undoing one's love. This is the best and wisest cure, for as long as love lasts there will be jealousy. Such was the fine imposed upon love by heaven. Where's Nise?
FINEA	By the fountain, with Laurencio.
OCTAVIO	What a tiresome business! I'll teach her to speak plainly and leave sonnets and lyrics alone. Time to put an end to their drivel!
	[Octavio leaves.]
FINEA	Who's to blame for my suffering? What happened just now? What did I see that inflames me so? Jealousy, my father says. What a terrible disease!

SCENE XIX

[Laurencio enters.]

LAURENCIO	*[Aside]* If I stay out of his way I won't annoy him, although I am grateful to him for interrupting Nise's scolding. But here are the eyes in which I bask. Lady.
FINEA	I shouldn't speak to you. Why did you go off with Nise?
LAURENCIO	I didn't go with her because I wanted to.
FINEA	Then why?
LAURENCIO	To annoy you.
FINEA	I suffer when I do not see you but, seeing you, I wish you were gone again. Fear and desire are dueling within me. I'm jealous of you. Oh, I know what jealousy is! My father has just told me its cruel name. He's also given me the remedy!

FINEA	Diga, señor padre:
	¿cómo llaman aquello que se siente
	cuando se va con otro lo que se ama?
OTAVIO	Ese agravio de amor, celos se llama.
FINEA	¿Celos?
OTAVIO	Pues, ¿no lo ves, que son sus hijos?

FINEA   El padre puede dar mil regocijos;   1810
        y es muy hombre de bien, mas desdichado
        en que tan malos hijos ha criado.

OTAVIO   *[Aparte]*
        Luz va tiniendo ya. Pienso y bien pienso
        que si amor la enseñase, aprendería.

FINEA   ¿Con qué se quita el mal de celosía?

OTAVIO   Con desenamorarse, si hay agravio,
        que es el remedio más prudente y sabio;
        que mientras hay amor ha de haber celos,
        pensión que dieron a este bien los cielos.
        ¿Adónde Nise está?

FINEA   Junto a la fuente   1820
        con Laurencio se fue.

OTAVIO   ¡Cansada cosa!
        Aprenda noramala a hablar su prosa,
        déjese de sonetos y canciones;
        allá voy a romperle las razones.   *[Váyase.]*

FINEA   ¿Por quién, en el mundo, pasa
        esto que pasa por mí?
        ¿Qué vi denantes, qué vi,
        que así me enciende y me abrasa?
        Celos dice el padre mío
        que son. ¡Brava enfermedad!   1830

ESCENA XIX

[Entre Laurencio.—Finea]

LAURENCIO   *[Aparte]*
        (Huyendo su autoridad,
        de enojarle me desvío;
        aunque, en parte, le agradezco
        que estorbase los enojos
        de Nise. Aquí están los ojos
        a cuyos rayos me ofrezco.)
        ¿Señora? . . .

FINEA   Estoy por no hablarte.
        ¿Cómo te fuiste con Nise?

LAURENCIO Which is?

FINEA To undo my love! Only by casting out love shall I find peace.

LAURENCIO And how will you accomplish this?

FINEA The person who planted love in me will know best how to uproot it.

LAURENCIO There's a better remedy.

FINEA What?

LAURENCIO Those who are approaching will help us in the cure.

SCENE XX

[Pedro, Duardo, and Feniso enter.]

PEDRO Laurencio and Finea are together.

FENISO He's taken leave of his senses!

LAURENCIO I welcome the three of you to the most joyful moment of my life. Since the wise Nise seems disposed to favor the two of you, listen now to the remedy I've concocted with Finea.

DUARDO It would seem, to see you flying about the house, that you're bewitched by Circe. We never see you outside.

LAURENCIO I have a scheme for making gold by alchemy.

PEDRO You are wasting health and your time, sir; pursuit of the impossible is exhausting.

LAURENCIO Be quiet, fool!

PEDRO The title is enough to guarantee my talking forever; fools are never silent.

LAURENCIO Excuse me while I talk to Finea.

DUARDO He's off again!

LAURENCIO I was speaking to the three of them, Finea, about the remedy you are seeking.

LAURENCIO   No me fui porque yo quise.

FINEA   Pues, ¿por qué?

LAURENCIO   Por no enojarte.   1840

FINEA   Pésame si no te veo,
             y en viéndote ya querría
             que te fueses, y a porfía
             anda el temor y el deseo.
                 Yo estoy celosa de ti;
             que ya sé lo que son celos;
             que su duro nombre, ¡ay cielos!,
             me dijo mi padre aquí;
                 mas también me dio el remedio.

LAURENCIO   ¿Cuál es?

FINEA   Desenamorarme;   1850
             porque podré sosegarme
             quitando el amor de en medio.

LAURENCIO   Pues eso, ¿cómo ha de ser?

FINEA   El que me puso el amor
             me le quitará mejor.

LAURENCIO   Un remedio suele haber.

FINEA   ¿Cuál?

LAURENCIO   Los que vienen aquí
             al remedio ayudarán.

ESCENA XX

[Entren Pedro, Duardo y Feniso.—Dichos]

PEDRO   Finea y Laurencio están
             juntos.

FENISO   Y él fuera de sí.   1860

LAURENCIO   Seáis los tres bien venidos
             a la ocasión más gallarda
             que se me pudo ofrecer;
             y pues de los dos el alma
             a sola Nise discreta
             inclina las esperanzas,
             oíd lo que con Finea
             para mi remedio pasa.

DUARDO   En esta casa parece,
             según por los aires andas,   1870
             que te ha dado hechizos Circe:
             nunca sales de esta casa.

FINEA   Undo my love, for jealousy is killing me!

LAURENCIO   If you were to declare before these gentlemen that you give
                 me your hand and swear to be my wife, all your jealousy will
                 vanish!

FINEA   Is that all? I'll do it!

LAURENCIO   Then you yourself call them over.

FINEA   Feniso, Duardo, Pedro.

THE THREE   M'lady.

FINEA   I swear to be Laurencio's wife.

DUARDO   Will wonders never cease!

LAURENCIO   Will you be witnesses of this?

THE THREE   Yes.

LAURENCIO   [To Finea] Know then, that you have just been cured of the love
                 and jealousy which troubled you.

FINEA   God bless you, Laurencio.

LAURENCIO   Will the three of you come with me to my home? A notary is
                 waiting for me there.

FENISO   So you're marrying Finea?

LAURENCIO   That's right, Feniso.

FENISO   And what of the lovely Nise?

LAURENCIO   I've changed intelligence into silver.

[Laurencio, Feniso, Duardo, and Pedro leave Finea alone.]

SCENE XXI

[Enter Nise and Octavio.]

NISE   I was making small talk with him, that's all!

LAURENCIO	Yo voy con mi pensamiento
	haciendo una rica traza
	para hacer oro de alquimia.
PEDRO	La salud y el tiempo gastas.
	Igual sería, señor,
	cansarte, pues todo cansa,
	de pretender imposibles.
LAURENCIO	¡Calla, necio!
PEDRO	El nombre basta
	para no callar jamás;
	que nunca los necios callan.
LAURENCIO	Aguardadme mientras hablo
	a Finea.
DUARDO	Parte.
LAURENCIO	Hablaba,
	Finea hermosa, a los tres,
	para el remedio que aguardas.
FINEA	¡Quítame presto el amor,
	que con sus celos me mata!
LAURENCIO	Si dices delante destos
	cómo me das la palabra
	de ser mi esposa y mujer,
	todos los celos se acaban.
FINEA	¿Eso no más? Yo lo haré.
LAURENCIO	Pues tú misma a los tres llama.
FINEA	¡Feniso, Düardo, Pedro!
LOS TRES	¡Señora!
FINEA	Yo doy palabra
	de ser esposa y mujer
	de Laurencio.
DUARDO	¡Cosa extraña!
LAURENCIO	¿Sois testigos desto?
LOS TRES	Sí.
LAURENCIO	Pues haz cuenta que estás sana
	del amor y de los celos
	que tanta pena te daban.
FINEA	¡Dios te lo pague, Laurencio!
LAURENCIO	Venid los tres a mi casa;
	que tengo un notario allí.
FENISO	Pues, ¿con Finea te casas?
LAURENCIO	Sí, Feniso.

1880

1890

1900

OCTAVIO	Beware, child, for these parleys may lead to more dishonor than you have honor to counteract.
NISE	He's an honest man, devoted to good literature, and I hold him for a master!
OCTAVIO	Juan Latino of Granada was not so fair, being the son of a slave of the Duke of Sessa, that it prevented him from marrying a daughter of one of the City Fathers, whose teacher he was. She studied grammar under him and he taught her to conjugate all right, when they came to the *amo, amas, amat!*
NISE	I am protected from such a fate by being your daughter.
FINEA	Gossiping about me?
OCTAVIO	Was this nitwit here all the time?!
FINEA	You have no cause to scold me.
OCTAVIO	Who's talking to you? Who is scolding you?
FINEA	You and Nise. Well, I'll have you know that Laurencio has just rid me of my love and left me as unblemished as the palm of my hand.
OCTAVIO	Now what! *[Aside]* Another idiocy!
FINEA	He told me that if I gave my word to be his wife before some witnesses, all my love would be undone. So, I gave it to him and now I'm cured of love and jealousy.
OCTAVIO	Monstrous! Nise, this girl will be the death of me!
NISE	You mean to say you gave your word? Don't you realize that you're already engaged?
FINEA	What difference does that make, it undid my love.
OCTAVIO	I bar Laurencio from this house! Forever!
NISE	Now that's wrong too! Laurencio is simply tricking her! He and Liseo both do it to teach her!
OCTAVIO	In that case I'll say no more.

FENISO   ¿Y Nise bella?

LAURENCIO   Troqué discreción por plata.

ESCENA XXI

[Quede Finea sola, y entren Nise y Otavio.]

NISE   Hablando estaba con él
              cosas de poca importancia.   1910

OTAVIO   Mira, hija, que estas cosas
              más deshonor que honor causan.

NISE   Es un honesto mancebo
              que de buenas letras trata,
              y téngole por maestro.

OTAVIO   No era tan blanco en Granada
              Juan Latino, que la hija
              de un Veinticuatro enseñaba;
              y siendo negro y esclavo,
              porque fue su madre esclava   1920
              del claro Duque de Sessa,
              honor de España y de Italia,
              se vino a casar con ella;
              que Gramática estudiaba,
              y la enseñó a conjugar
              en llegando al *amo, amas;*
              que así llama el matrimonio
              el latín.

NISE   De eso me guarda
              ser tu hija.

FINEA   ¿Murmuráis
              de mis cosas?

OTAVIO   ¿Aquí estaba   1930
              esta loca?

FINEA   Ya no es tiempo
              de reñirme.

OTAVIO   ¿Quién te habla?,
              ¿quién te riñe?

FINEA   Nise y tú.
              Pues sepan que agora acaba
              de quitarme el amor todo
              Laurencio, como la palma.

OTAVIO   *[Aparte]*
              ¿Hay alguna bobería?

FINEA   Díjome que se quitaba
              el amor con que le diese

FINEA   Oh! So just like that, you lock me up!

OCTAVIO   Come with me

FINEA   Where?

OCTAVIO   To the nearest notary.

FINEA   Let's go.

OCTAVIO   Come along. Oh, the peace I enjoy in my old age!

             [Exit Octavio and Finea leaving Nise alone.]

NISE   Laurencio told me that he and Liseo have taken this tack to see
             if they can polish her rough edges. It strikes me well.

SCENE XXII

[Enter Liseo.]

LISEO   Wisest Nise, did Laurencio tell you of my love?

NISE   What did you say? Are you dreaming or raving?

LISEO   Laurencio pledged to aid me in my hopes now that I've chosen
             to center them on you.

NISE   I believe you must be tired of talking to your bride; or else
             the blade of your wit has become nicked and dull by the
             roughness of the wood upon which you carve, and now you
             come to sharpen and hone it on me so you can return to
             carve upon her!

LISEO   My love for you trades in truths, not jests.

NISE   Are you mad?

LISEO   When I thought of marrying one who was thought to be so—
             yes! I have since transferred my affection.

NISE   What irritation, inconstancy, madness, error, and treason to my
             father and my sister! Leave me this instant!

	de su mujer la palabra;	1940
	y delante de testigos	
	se la he dado, y estoy sana	
	del amor y de los celos.	
OTAVIO	¡Esto es cosa temeraria!	
	Ésta, Nise, ha de quitarme	
	la vida.	
NISE	¿Palabra dabas	
	de mujer a ningún hombre?	
	¿No sabes que estás casada?	
FINEA	¿Para quitarme el amor,	
	qué importa?	
OTAVIO	No entre en mi casa	1950
	Laurencio más.	
NISE	Es error,	
	porque Laurencio la engaña:	
	que él y Liseo lo dicen	
	no más de para enseñarla.	
OTAVIO	De esa manera, yo callo.	
FINEA	¡Oh! Pues, ¿con eso nos tapa	
	la boca?	
OTAVIO	Vente conmigo.	
FINEA	¿A dónde?	
OTAVIO	Donde te aguarda	
	un notario.	
FINEA	Vamos.	
OTAVIO	Ven.	
	[Aparte]	
	¡Qué descanso de mis canas! *[Vanse.]*	1960
	[Nise sola]	
NISE	Hame contado Laurencio	
	que han tomado aquesta traza	
	Liseo y él, para ver	
	si aquella rudeza labran,	
	y no me parece mal.	

ESCENA XXII

[Entre Liseo.—Nise]

LISEO	¿Hate contado mis ansias
	Laurencio, discreta Nise?
NISE	¿Qué me dices? ¿Sueñas o hablas?

LISEO   Is this the way to repay the wildness of my love?

NISE   If it be wild, enough said!

Scene XXIII

[Enter Laurencio.]

LAURENCIO   *[Aside]* They are talking alone. If Liseo has declared himself, then Nise knows my flattery was false. She's seen me!

NISE   *[As though to Liseo]* Oh! You glorious answer to my hopes!

LISEO   I, answer your hopes, Lady?

NISE   Even though they say you are unfaithful, my heart refuses to believe it!

LISEO   Unfaithful to you, Nise? If ever I show love for your sister, may I be struck by lightning.

LAURENCIO   *[Aside]* She aims her remarks at me and Liseo presumes that she's flattering him.

NISE   I must go! A love of such force robs me of my reason that I'll begin to rave!

LISEO   Oh, don't leave, Nise! After granting me such favors, you'll kill me if you snatch them away!

NISE   Let me go.   *[Nise leaves.]*

Scene XXIV

LISEO   Were you behind my back all this time?

LAURENCIO   I just came in.

LISEO   Then it was to you that ungrateful but discreet woman was talking—while she pretended to talk to me!

LISEO	Palabra me dio Laurencio	
	de ayudar mis esperanzas,	1970
	viendo que las pongo en ti.	

NISE   Pienso que de hablar te cansas
con tu esposa, o que se embota
en la dureza que labras
el cuchillo de tu gusto,
y, para volver a hablarla,
quieres darle un filo en mí.

LISEO   Verdades son las que trata
contigo mi amor, no burlas.

NISE   ¿Estás loco?

LISEO   Quien pensaba   1980
casarse con quien lo era,
de pensarlo ha dado causa.
Yo he mudado pensamiento.

NISE   ¡Qué necedad, qué inconstancia,
qué locura, error, traición
a mi padre y a mi hermana!
¡Id en buen hora, Liseo!

LISEO   ¿Desa manera me pagas
tan desatinado amor?

NISE   Pues, si es desatino, ¡basta!   1990

ESCENA XXIII

[Entre Laurencio.—Dichos]

LAURENCIO   *[Aparte]*
Hablando están los dos solos.
Si Liseo se declara,
Nise ha de saber también
que mis lisonjas la engañan.
Creo que me ha visto ya.

[Nise dice, como que habla con Liseo.]

NISE   ¡Oh gloria de mi esperanza!

LISEO   ¿Yo vuestra gloria, señora?

NISE   Aunque dicen que me tratas
con traición, yo no lo creo;
que no lo consiente el alma.   2000

LISEO   ¿Traición, Nise? ¡Si en mi vida
mostrare amor a tu hermana,
me mate un rayo del cielo!

LAURENCIO   Don't fret. Stones are worn down by the flow of water! I'll
            arrange it so that tonight you will be able to talk to her in my
            name. This is a very learned woman, Liseo; you won't divert
            her mind from the impossibility it entertains unless you trick
            her into it. And, remember, I belong to Finea.

LISEO   Procure me a remedy or I'll go mad!

LAURENCIO   Rest easy and leave the remedy to me. To outwit a learned
            woman is the greatest victory of all.

End of Act II—*Lady Nitwit*

LAURENCIO	*[Aparte]*
	Es conmigo con quien habla
	Nise, y presume Liseo
	que le requiebra y regala.
NISE	Quiérome quitar de aquí;
	que con tal fuerza me engaña
	amor, que diré locuras.
LISEO	No os vais, ¡oh Nise gallarda!; 2010
	que después de los favores
	quedará sin vida el alma.
NISE	¡Dejadme pasar! *[Vase.]*

ESCENA XXIV

LISEO	¿Aquí
	estabas a mis espaldas?
LAURENCIO	Agora entré.
LISEO	¿Luego a ti
	te hablaba y te requebraba,
	aunque me miraba a mí,
	aquella discreta ingrata?
LAURENCIO	No tengas pena; las piedras
	ablanda el curso del agua. 2020
	Yo sabré hacer que esta noche
	puedas, en mi nombre, hablarla.
	Ésta es discreta, Liseo.
	No podrás, si no la engañas,
	quitalla del pensamiento
	el imposible que aguarda;
	porque yo soy de Finea.
LISEO	Si mi remedio no trazas,
	cuéntame loco de amor.
LAURENCIO	Déjame el remedio, y calla; 2030
	porque burlar un discreto
	es la vitoria más alta.

Fin del segundo acto de *La dama boba*.

ACT THREE
ACTO TERCERO

ACTO TERCERO

ESCENA I

[Sala en casa de Otavio.]

[Finea sola]

FINEA   ¡Amor, divina invención
de conservar la belleza
de nuestra naturaleza,
o accidente o elección!
Extraños efetos son
los que de tu ciencia nacen,
pues las tinieblas deshacen,
pues hacen hablar los mudos,   2040
pues los ingenios más rudos
sabios y discretos hacen.
    No ha dos meses que vivía
a las bestias tan igual,
que aun el alma racional
parece que no tenía.
Con el animal sentía
y crecía con la planta;
la razón divina y santa
estaba eclipsada en mí,   2050
hasta que en tus rayos vi,
a cuyo sol se levanta.
    Tú desataste y rompiste
la escuridad de mi ingenio;
tú fuiste el divino genio
que me enseñaste, y me diste
la luz con que me pusiste
el nuevo ser en que estoy.
Mil gracias, amor, te doy,
pues me enseñaste tan bien,   2060
que dicen cuantos me ven
que tan diferente soy.
    A pura imaginación
de la fuerza de un deseo,
en los palacios me veo
de la divina razón.
¡Tanto la contemplación

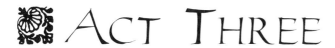 Act Three

Scene I

[Room in Octavio's house.]
[Finea alone.]

FINEA   Whether by chance or choice, love is the most heavenly invention for preserving the beauty of our natures. What wondrous effects are born, Love, of your science! You dispel the mists of the mind, give speech to the mute, and transform the witless into wits of discretion. Two months ago, no more, I lived so like a beast I lacked the power of reason. I thought like a beast and grew like a plant, my reason was eclipsed until your rays, like those of the rising sun, fell upon me. You expelled the darkness of my mind and became my heavenly master, shedding light that led me to my new and present self. I give you, Love, a thousand thanks. You've taught me so well that all who behold me marvel at my transformation. By sheer strength of imagining desire I have made my way to the palace of reason. Such is the power of Love! However, it's high time, Love, to honor me with a degree. Invest me with Laurencio who, with your help, has taught me well.

Scene II

[Clara enters.]

CLARA   You should hear the hubbub you're causing with your new-found reason.

FINEA   I'm glad it pleases my father.

CLARA   He's boasting to Miseno at this very moment about how you read, and write, and dance! He claims you have a new soul in your body, but he attributes the miracle to your love for Liseo.

de un bien pudo levantarme!
Ya puedes del grado honrarme,
dándome a Laurencio, amor,   2070
con quien pudiste mejor,
enamorada, enseñarme.

ESCENA II

[Clara.—Finea]

CLARA   En grande conversación
             están de tu entendimiento.

FINEA   Huélgome que esté contento
             mi padre en esta ocasión.

CLARA   Hablando está con Miseno
             de cómo lees, escribes
             y danzas; dice que vives
             con otra alma en cuerpo ajeno.   2080
                Atribúyele al amor
             de Liseo este milagro.

FINEA   En otras aras consagro
             mis votos, Clara, mejor:
                Laurencio ha sido el maestro.

CLARA   Como Pedro lo fue mío.

FINEA   De verlos hablar me río
             en este milagro nuestro.
                ¡Gran fuerza tiene el amor,
             catedrático divino!   2090

ESCENA III

[Miseno y Otavio]

MISENO   Yo pienso que es el camino
             de su remedio mejor.
                Y ya, pues habéis llegado
             a ver con entendimiento
             a Finea, que es contento
             nunca de vos esperado,
                a Nise podéis casar
             con este mozo gallardo.

OTAVIO   Vos solamente a Düardo
             pudiérades abonar.   2100
                Mozuelo me parecía
             destos que se desvanecen,
             a quien agora enloquecen

FINEA   I worship at another shrine, as you know. Laurencio was my
            mentor.

CLARA   As Pedro was mine.

FINEA   Hearing them talk so much of our miracle makes me laugh. Ah,
            the power of Love; indeed, he's a doctor of divinity.

SCENE III

[Enter Miseno and Octavio.]

MISENO   Things are looking up! Since Finea seems to have acquired
            some understanding, a blessing you never anticipated, you are
            now free to marry Nise to this handsome young man.

OCTAVIO   I wouldn't listen to praise of Duardo from anyone but you! He
            struck me as one of those addlepated boys alternately mad-
            dened by arrogance and poetry. It takes more than sonnets to
            make a husband! Nise's touched!—academically deified, and
            she draws these silly boys home like flies! What business does
            a woman have dabbling in Petrarch and Garcilaso, when her
            Virgil and Tasso should be weaving, sewing, and embroidery? I
            saw her library yesterday, and the titles read something like
            this: *A Tale of Two Lovers* taken from the Greek, *Rimas* by Lope
            de Vega, *Galatea* by Cervantes, *Os Lusiadas* by Camões, *The
            Shepherds of Bethlehem* by Lope de Vega, *Plays* by Guillén de
            Castro, *Lyrics* by Ochoa, *Poem* read by Luis Vélez at the
            Academy of the Duke of Pastrana, *Works* of Luque, *Letters* of
            Juan de Arguijo, *One Hundred Sonnets* by Liñán, *Works* of the
            divine Herrera, *The Pilgrim in His Country* by Lope de Vega, and
            that picaresque novel by Alemán! Ooof! Upon my life, I wear
            you out! And to tell the truth, I wanted to burn them all!

MISENO   Marry her off! You'll see how entertained she'll be with preg-
            nancies and babies.

OCTAVIO   Delightful chores! Now, if Duardo has a touch of the poet about
            him, we could marry them right away.

la arrogancia y la poesía.
   No son gracias de marido
sonetos. Nise es tentada
de académica endiosada,
que a casa los ha traído.
   ¿Quién le mete a una mujer
con Petrarca y Garcilaso,   2110
siendo su Virgilio y Taso
hilar, labrar y coser?
   Ayer sus librillos vi,
papeles y escritos varios;
pensé que devocionarios,
y desta suerte leí:
   Historia de dos amantes,
sacada de lengua griega;
Rimas, de Lope de Vega;
Galatea, de Cervantes;   2120
   el *Camões* de Lisboa,
Los pastores de Belén,
Comedias de don Guillén
de Castro, *Liras* de Ochoa;
   Canción que Luis Vélez dijo
en la academia del duque
de Pastrana; *Obras* de Luque;
Cartas de don Juan de Arguijo;
   Cien sonetos de Liñán,
Obras de Herrera el divino,   2130
el libro del *Peregrino,*
y *El pícaro,* de Alemán.
   Mas, ¿qué os canso? Por mi vida,
que se los quise quemar.

MISENO   Casalda y veréisla estar
ocupada y divertida
   en el parir y el criar.

OTAVIO   ¡Qué gentiles devociones!
Si Düardo hace canciones,
bien los podemos casar.   2140

MISENO   Es poeta caballero,
no temáis; hará por gusto
versos.

OTAVIO   Con mucho disgusto
los de Nise considero.
   Temo, y en razón lo fundo,
si en esto da, que ha de haber
un don Quijote mujer
que dé que reír al mundo.

MISENO   Never fear, he's a gentleman and composes verses only for his
                  own amusement.

OCTAVIO   Nise's poems rouse my spleen, I can tell you! If she persists
                  in this, the world will soon be laughing at a Don Quixote in
                  petticoats!

SCENE IV

[Liseo, Nise, and Turín enter.]

LISEO   You treat me with such disdain that I'm thinking of appealing
                  to another court where my affection will be judged more favor-
                  ably. Remember, Nise, that Finea is under lien to me; and a love
                  as spurned as mine may well seek comfort in her. I underesti-
                  mated your disdain, which seems to grow apace with my love
                  and thrives on my devotion! Finea's understanding has under-
                  gone such a transformation that it may rekindle the fury of my
                  love. So, treat me well, Nise, lest I appeal my love in Finea's
                  court.

NISE   Your threats would be well advised, had I ever loved you.

LISEO   A nobleman, a gentleman such as I, should be held in more
                  esteem, and not unworthy of affection!

NISE   Love lives where you find it. It's not a question of choice, it's
                  an accident; and one finds it where one feels it, and not where
                  it reasonably should be. Love is not a quality, but rather the
                  configuration of the stars, which mold the wills that will be
                  one.

LISEO   I am not prompted by jealousy when I tell you it is not fair,
                  m'lady, to blame the heavens for the lowness of one's taste!
                  Errors should not be blamed on the stars!

NISE   I do not accuse them. Laurencio is a nobleman who could well
                  honor . . .

LISEO   Stop.

ESCENA IV

[Entren Liseo y Nise y Turín.—Dichos]

LISEO	Trátasme con tal desdén,	
	que pienso que he de apelar	2150
	adonde sepan tratar	
	mis obligaciones bien;	
	pues advierte, Nise bella,	
	que Finea ya es sagrado;	
	que un amor tan desdeñado	
	puede hallar remedio en ella.	
	Tu desdén, que imaginé	
	que pudiera ser menor,	
	crece al paso de mi amor,	
	medra al lado de mi fe;	2160
	y su corto entendimiento	
	ha llegado a tal mudanza,	
	que puede dar esperanza	
	a mi loco pensamiento.	
	Pues, Nise, trátame bien;	
	u de Finea el favor	
	será sala en que mi amor	
	apele de tu desdén.	
NISE	Liseo, el hacerme fieros	
	fuera bien considerado	2170
	cuando yo te hubiera amado.	
LISEO	Los nobles y caballeros	
	como yo, se han de estimar,	
	no lo indigno de querer.	
NISE	El amor se ha de tener	
	adonde se puede hallar;	
	que como no es elección,	
	sino sólo un accidente,	
	tiénese donde se siente,	
	no donde fuera razón.	2180
	El amor no es calidad,	
	sino estrellas que conciertan	
	las voluntades que aciertan	
	a ser una voluntad.	
LISEO	Eso, señora, no es justo;	
	y no lo digo con celos,	
	que pongáis culpa a los cielos	
	de la bajeza del gusto.	
	A lo que se hace mal,	
	no es bien decir: «Fue mi estrella.»	2190

NISE   Stop? I insist that you give him his due!

LISEO   Were your father not near . . .

OCTAVIO   Ah, Liseo!

LISEO   Yes, sir!

NISE   *[Aside]* What singular behavior! As though he could take my
            love by storm!

SCENE V

[Celia enters.]

CELIA   The dancing master is here for the lesson.

OCTAVIO   He couldn't have come at a better time. Go call the musicians.
            I want Miseno to see for himself the change that's come over
            Finea.

LISEO   *[Aside]* Betrayed, oh love of mine, it's time to return to Finea.
            Disguised as revenge, love often shifts allegiances, wisely, from
            disdain to favor.

CELIA   Here are the musicians.

SCENE VI

[Musician and the Dancing Master enter.]

OCTAVIO   Welcome.

LISEO   *[Aside]* Today's my day for revenge.

OCTAVIO   Nise and Finea.

NISE   Sir.

OCTAVIO   Let's have that dance you did the other day.

NISE   Yo no pongo culpa en ella,
          ni en el curso celestial;
             porque Laurencio es un hombre
          tan hidalgo y caballero
          que puede honrar . . .

LISEO   ¡Paso!

NISE   Quiero
          que reverenciéis su nombre.

LISEO   A no estar tan cerca Otavio . . .

OTAVIO   ¡Oh, Liseo!

LISEO   ¡Oh, mi señor!

NISE   *[Aparte]*
          ¡Qué se ha de tener amor
          por fuerza! ¡Notable agravio!   2200

ESCENA V

[Entre Celia.—Dichos]

CELIA   El maestro de danzar
          a las dos llama a lición.

OTAVIO   Él viene a buena ocasión.
          Vaya un criado a llamar
             los músicos, porque vea
          Miseno a lo que ha llegado
          Finea.

ESCENA VI

[Músicos.—Dichos]

LISEO   *[Aparte]* Amor, engañado,
          hoy volveréis a Finea;
             que muchas veces amor,
          disfrazado en la venganza,   2210
          hace una justa mudanza
          desde un desdén a un favor.

CELIA   Los músicos y él venían.
          [Entren los Músicos.]

OTAVIO   ¡Muy bien venidos seáis!

LISEO   *[Aparte]*
          ¡Hoy, pensamientos, vengáis
          los agravios que os hacían!

OTAVIO   Nise y Finea . . .

NISE   ¡Señor! . . .

LISEO   *[Aside]* Love is all inconstancy!

[Octavio, Miseno, and Liseo seat themselves; the Musicians sing, and the two sisters dance to all or a portion of the following.]

I

Weary of courting greedy maidens
Who, seeing him naked and poor,
Let him starve and beg and shiver,
Love took a ship and sailed away
Away, away to the Indies.

His wounded hearts weren't worth a sneeze
To pay love's way to the Indies.
He sold his arrows, bow, and quiver
For money to pay his way,
To pay his way to the Indies.
In the Indies he learned a trade,
One that made profit in silver.
Carrying letters and billet-doux,
He became the richest of pimps.
Away, away in the Indies.
Then back he came across the seas!
Laden with jewels, silver, and gold,
Turned out in elegant linens;
Oh how the maidens surrendered
To Love come back from the Indies!
Dandied out in ribbons and silk
He stormed and assaulted Madrid.
The women squealed and cried with joy,
"Who can he be? What is his name?
This handsome man from the Indies?"

II

Where is he from? Where is he from?
He comes from Panama.
Where are you from my gentleman?
He comes from Panama.
Hat band covered with gold and jewels!
He comes from Panama.
A golden chain around your neck!

OTAVIO   Vaya aquí, por vida mía,
         el baile del otro día.

LISEO   *[Aparte]*
         ¡Todo es mudanzas amor!   2220

         [Otavio, Miseno y Liseo se sienten; los Músicos canten,
         y las dos bailen ansí.]

         I
            Amor, cansado de ver
         tanto interés en las damas,
         y que, por desnudo y pobre,
         ninguna favor le daba,
         pasóse a las Indias,
         vendió el aljaba,
         que más quiere doblones
         que vidas y almas.
            Trató en las Indias Amor,
         no en joyas, sedas y holandas,   2230
         sino en ser sutil tercero
         de billetes y de cartas.
         Volvió de las Indias
         con oro y plata;
         que el Amor bien vestido
         rinde las damas.
            Paseó la corte Amor
         con mil cadenas y bandas;
         las damas, como le vían,
         desta manera le hablan: 2240

         II
         ¿De dó viene, de dó viene?
         —Viene de Panamá.—

         ¿De dó viene el caballero?
         —Viene de Panamá.—
         Trancelín en el sombrero,
         —Viene de Panamá.—
         cadenita de oro al cuello,
         —Viene de Panamá.—
         en los brazos el grig[u]iesco,
         —Viene de Panamá.—   2250
         las ligas con rapacejos,
         —Viene de Panamá.—
         zapatos al uso nuevo,
         —Viene de Panamá.—
         sotanilla a lo turquesco.
         —Viene de Panamá.—

         ¿De dó viene, de dó viene?
         —Viene de Panamá.—

He comes from Panama.
With billowing sleeves all puffed out.
He comes from Panama.
Garters and buckles flecked with gold.
He comes from Panama.
Polished and shining square-toed shoes.
He comes from Panama.
Sporting a cloak of Turkish cut
He comes from Panama.

Where are you from? Where are you from?
He comes from Panama.

III

Where does the nobleman come from?
He comes from Panama.
Narrow his collar, long his sleeves.
He comes from Panama.
Wearing a dagger in his sash.
He comes from Panama.
His gloves are reeking of perfume.
He comes from Panama.
He rhymes and puns par excellence.
He comes from Panama.
Free with his smiles, tight with his purse.
He comes from Panama.
How rash, and rude, and insulting.
He comes from Panama.
Claims to be Love from the Indies.
He comes from Panama.
A bumpkin fop from the Indies?
He comes from Panama.
Pretending to be a Spaniard.
He comes from Panama.

Where is he from? You know where!
He comes from Panama.

IV

How dashing, Love with all his gold!
Generosity does the trick.

III

¿De dó viene el hijo de algo?
—Viene de Panamá.—   2260
Corto cuello y puños largos,
—Viene de Panamá.—
la daga en banda colgando,
—Viene de Panamá.—
guante de ámbar adobado,
—Viene de Panamá.—
gran jugador del vocablo,
—Viene de Panamá.—
no da dinero y da manos,
—Viene de Panamá.—   2270
enfadoso y mal criado;
—Viene de Panamá.—
es Amor, llámase indiano,
—Viene de Panamá.—
es chapetón castellano,
—Viene de Panamá.—
en criollo disfrazado.
—Viene de Panamá.—
¿De dó viene, de dó viene?
—Viene de Panamá.—   2280

IV

    ¡Oh, qué bien parece Amor
con las cadenas y galas!
Que sólo el dar enamora,
porque es cifra de las gracias.
Niñas, doncellas y viejas
van a buscarle a su casa,
más importunas que moscas,
en viendo que hay miel de plata.
Sobre cuál le ha de querer,
de vivos celos se abrasan,   2290
y alrededor de su puerta
unas tras otras le cantan:

V

    ¡Deja las avellanicas, moro,
que yo me las varearé.
El Amor se ha vuelto godo,
—Que yo me las varearé.—
puños largos, cuello corto,
—Que yo me las varearé.—
sotanilla y liga de oro,
—Que yo me las varearé.—   2300
sombrero y zapato romo,
—Que yo me las varearé.—

Hiding the pock marks on his face,
Gold is the finest cosmetic!
Gold's to be had in the Indies!
Girls, and maidens, and dried up hags,
They flock to his house by the score;
Drawn like flies by golden honey,
A tempting sweet they all adore
Imported straight from the Indies.
All of them burn with jealousy,
Fights for his favors are endless.
Oh how they swarm and push and shout,
Clamoring loudly at his door,
For love of Gold from the Indies!

V

Leave a few nuts upon the tree,
And I will knock them down.
Love is claiming a family tree.
And I will knock them down.
Short collar and wide of cuffs.
And I will knock them down.
A cloak and a golden garter.
And I will knock them down.
With square-peaked hat and blunt-toed shoe.
And I will knock them down.
Narrow breeches, wide full sleeves.
And I will knock them down.
Spending nothing and talking much.
And I will knock them down.
Really old, pretends to be young.
And I will knock them down.
Coward and braggart both at once.
And I will knock them down.
But now he's gazing right at me.
And I will knock them down?

Madness of love! Madness of love!
And I will knock them down?
I'm for you, you're for another!
And I will knock them down!

> *manga ancha, calzón angosto.*
> *—Que yo me las varearé.—*
> *Él habla mucho y da poco,*
> *—Que yo me las varearé.—*
> *es viejo, y dice que es mozo,*
> *—Que yo me las varearé.—*
> *es cobarde, y matamoros.*
> *—Que yo me las varearé.—*   2310
> *Ya se descubrió los ojos.*
> *—Que yo me las varearé.—*
> *¡Amor loco y amor loco!*
> *—Que yo me las varearé.—*
> *¡Yo por vos, y vos por otro!*
> *—Que yo me las varearé.—*
>
> *Deja las avellanicas, moro,*
> *que yo me las varearé.*

MISENO   ¡Gallardamente, por cierto!
            Dad gracias al cielo, Otavio,   2320
            que os satisfizo el agravio.

OTAVIO   Hagamos este concierto
                de Düardo con [Nise].
            Hijas, yo tengo que hablaros.

FINEA   Yo nací para agradaros.

OTAVIO   ¿Quién hay que mi dicha crea?

ESCENA VII

[Éntrense todos, y queden allí Liseo y Turín.]

LISEO   Oye, Turín.

TURÍN   ¿Qué me quieres?

LISEO   Quiérote comunicar
            un nuevo gusto.

TURÍN   Si es dar
            sobre tu amor pareceres,   2330
                busca un letrado de amor.

LISEO   Yo he mudado parecer.

TURÍN   A ser dejar de querer
            a Nise, fuera el mejor.

LISEO   El mismo; porque Finea
            me ha de vengar de su agravio.

TURÍN   No te tengo por tan sabio
            que tal discreción te crea.

LISEO   De nuevo quiero tratar
            mi casamiento. Allá voy.   2340

> Leave a few nuts upon the tree,
> And I will knock them down.

MISENO   Most graceful, indeed! Octavio, you can thank heaven your thorn bush has finally blossomed!

OCTAVIO   Let's settle the matter of Duardo and Nise. Daughters, I have something to discuss with you.

FINEA   I was born to give you pleasure.

OCTAVIO   Oh, my good fortune! Who'd believe it!

SCENE VII

[They leave. Liseo and Turín remain.]

LISEO   Oh, Turín.

TURÍN   What do you wish?

LISEO   To make you privy to my new desire.

TURÍN   If you want an opinion on your love, go to an expert.

LISEO   I have changed my mind.

TURÍN   Short of discarding your affection for Nise, nothing could be better.

LISEO   My very thought! Finea is going to avenge my wrongs.

TURÍN   You haven't shown yourself wise enough, so far, to make me believe that.

LISEO   I'm off to renew my suit this very moment.

TURÍN   Then I'll second you.

LISEO   I'll be revenged this very day!

TURÍN   It never pays to marry for revenge. It would be perfectly sensible if you married Finea because she's lovely and has stumbled upon her brains. But as for Nise, I rather doubt her much fabled intelligence.

TURÍN	De tu parecer estoy.
LISEO	Hoy me tengo de vengar.
TURÍN	Nunca ha de ser el casarse

TURÍN   Nunca ha de ser el casarse
por vengarse de un desdén;
que nunca se casó bien
quien se casó por vengarse.
   Porque es gallarda Finea
y porque el seso cobró
—pues de Nise no sé yo
que tan entendida sea—,   2350
   será bien casarte luego.

LISEO   Miseno ha venido aquí.
Algo tratan contra mí.

TURÍN   Que lo mires bien te ruego.

LISEO   ¡No hay más! ¡A pedirla voy!

[Váyase Liseo.]

TURÍN   El cielo tus pasos guíe
y del error te desvíe
en que yo por Celia estoy.
   ¡Que enamore amor un hombre
como yo! ¡Amor desatina!   2360
¡Que una ninfa de cocina,
para blasón de su nombre,
   ponga: «Aquí murió Turín
entre sartenes y cazos»!

ESCENA VIII

[Laurencio y Pedro.—Turín]

LAURENCIO   Todo es poner embarazos
para que no llegue al fin.

PEDRO   ¡Habla bajo, que hay escuchas!

LAURENCIO   ¡Oh, Turín!

TURÍN   ¡Señor Laurencio . . . !

LAURENCIO   ¿Tanta quietud y silencio?

TURÍN   Hay obligaciones muchas   2370
para callar un discreto,
y yo muy discreto soy.

LAURENCIO   ¿Qué hay de Liseo?

TURÍN   A eso voy.
Fuese a casar.

PEDRO   ¡Buen secreto!

LISEO   Miseno has come again and I'm sure they're plotting against me.

TURIN   Keep an eye on him, I beg you.

LISEO   Well, that's that! I'm off to ask for her hand.

[Liseo leaves.]

TURÍN   May heaven guide your steps and lead you from the error I made with Celia. What! A man such as I, fall in love? Really! Love drives us mad! To think that a scullery nymph can now write upon its wall, "Here died Turín! Among the pots and pans!"

SCENE VIII

[Laurencio and Pedro enter.]

LAURENCIO   It all depends on being able to cause delays.

PEDRO   The walls have ears! Softly!

LAURENCIO   Oh, Turín!

TURÍN   Yes, sir.

LAURENCIO   Why so silent, so mute?

TURÍN   The wise have causes galore to keep their counsel—and I am very wise.

LAURENCIO   What of Liseo?

TURÍN   I was coming to that; he's gone off to get married.

PEDRO   So much for that secret!

TURÍN   He is so much in love with Finea, or else so determined to revenge himself on Nise, that he's sworn to be married today, and has gone to ask Octavio for Finea's hand.

LAURENCIO   I could take that as an insult.

TURÍN	Está tan enamorado
	de la señora Finea,
	si no es que venganza sea
	de Nise, que me ha jurado
	que luego se ha de casar.
	Y es ido a pedirla a Otavio.

2380

LAURENCIO ¿Podré yo llamarme a agravio?

TURÍN Pues, ¿él os puede agraviar?

LAURENCIO Las palabras, ¿suelen darse
para no cumplirlas?

TURÍN   No.

LAURENCIO De no casarse la dio.

TURÍN Él no la quiebra en casarse.

LAURENCIO ¿Cómo?

TURÍN   Porque él no se casa
con la que solía ser,
sino con otra mujer.

LAURENCIO ¿Cómo es otra?

TURÍN   Porque pasa   2390
del no saber al saber;
y con saber le obligó.
¿Mandáis otra cosa?

LAURENCIO   No.

TURÍN Pues adiós.   *[Vase.]*

ESCENA IX

LAURENCIO   ¿Qué puedo hacer?
¡Ay Pedro! Lo que temí
y tenía sospechado
del ingenio que ha mostrado
Finea, se cumple aquí.
    Como la ha visto Liseo
tan discreta, la afición   2400
ha puesto en la discreción.

PEDRO Y en el oro algún deseo.
    Cansóle la bobería,
la discreción le animó.

ESCENA X

[Entre Finea.—Dichos]

FINEA ¡Clara, Laurencio, me dio
nuevas de tanta alegría!

| TURÍN | In what way, pray? |

LAURENCIO Should one break one's word?

TURÍN   No.

LAURENCIO Well, he swore not to marry her.

TURÍN   He isn't breaking his word by marrying her.

LAURENCIO How so?

TURÍN   Because he's marrying an entirely different woman.

LAURENCIO How, different?

TURÍN   She's transformed! Having exchanged idiocy for intelligence, her wit won him over. May I be of further service?

LAURENCIO No.

TURÍN   Then, good day.   [Turín leaves.]

SCENE IX

LAURENCIO What am I to do? Ah, Pedro, my fears of Finea's improvement are falling due. Liseo has discovered her newfound wit and reversed his affection in that direction.

PEDRO   With some interest in her gold, I might add. Her idiocy exhausted him but her intelligence revives him.

SCENE X

[Finea enters.]

FINEA   Clara brought me the joyful tidings, and I left my father to come to you. But even if she'd kept the news from me, I have my private messengers. My soul beholds your image in a thousand crystals and follows you wherever you go! The memories you've left in these my eyes will live forever. The whole house

Luego a mi padre dejé,
y aunque ella me lo callara,
yo tengo quien me avisara,
que es el alma, que te ve   2410
   por mil vidros y cristales,
por donde quiera que vas,
porque en mis ojos estás
con memorias inmortales.
   Todo este grande lugar
tiene colgado de espejos
mi amor, juntos y parejos,
para poderte mirar.
   Si vuelvo el rostro allí, veo
tu imagen; si a estotra parte,   2320
también; y ansí viene a darte
nombre de sol mi deseo;
   que en cuantos espejos mira
y fuentes de pura plata,
su bello rostro retrata
y su luz divina espira.

LAURENCIO   ¡Ay Finea! ¡A Dios pluguiera
que nunca tu entendimiento
llegara, como ha llegado,
a la mundanza que veo!   2430
Necio, me tuvo seguro,
y sospechoso discreto;
porque yo no te quería
para pedirte consejo.
¿Qué libro esperaba yo
de tus manos? ¿En qué pleito
habías jamás de hacerme
información en derecho?
Inocente te quería,
porque una mujer cordero   2440
es tusón de su marido,
que puede traerla al pecho.
Todas sabéis lo que basta
para casada, a lo menos;
no hay mujer necia en el mundo,
porque el no hablar no es defeto.
Hable la dama en la reja,
escriba, diga concetos
en el coche, en el estrado,
de amor, de engaños, de celos;   2450
pero la casada sepa
de su familia el gobierno;
porque el más discreto hablar

is hung with mirrors of my love that I may dwell on you. When I gaze in that direction, I see your image; and over there, I see it once again! And so it is my desire proclaims you the sun—for like the sun, mirrors and fountains of pure silver capture your image and glow with your light.

LAURENCIO   Oh, Finea! Would to God your understanding had never flowered! I was secure in your simplicity, but your intelligence fills me with apprehension. I didn't fall in love with you to ask you for advice; I didn't expect you to write me a book! In what lawsuit would I have asked you to testify on my behalf? I loved you in your innocence; because a lamb of a woman is to her husband like the golden fleece, an honor to wear upon his breast. All women possess the wifely essentials, and no woman in the world would be criticized for being chary of words. Let young damsels talk at the grill of their windows; let them write and spout conceits of love, deception, and jealousy as they ride in their carriages or talk at their windows; but let a wife know how to govern her home; for, in a wife, the most elegant speech is less hallowed than silence. Just look at the trouble that's come on the heels of your transformation since—oh, what a plight!—since Liseo has now gone to ask for your hand again. He's abandoned your sister and is going now to marry you and I am going to die! Would to God you'd never learned to speak.

FINEA   Laurencio, how am I at fault? I learned all I know inspired by your virtues. Conquered by your compliments, I learned to talk in order to talk to you. I read books, the better to read your letters; I write in order to answer them. Love has been my teacher, love has made me learn, and you are the science I have mastered. What displeases you in this?

LAURENCIO   I bewail my own misfortune! However, since you have learned so much, m'lady, give me a remedy.

FINEA   The cure is easy.

LAURENCIO   How?

FINEA   If Liseo has come to love me because my nature has transformed itself into good sense, he will abhor me if it reverts to its former ignorance.

no es sancto como el silencio.
Mira el daño que me vino
de transformarse tu ingenio,
pues va a pedirte, ¡ay de mí!,
para su mujer, Liseo.
Ya deja a Nise, tu hermana.
Él se casa. Yo soy muerto.   2460
¡Nunca, plega a Dios, hablaras!

FINEA   ¿De qué me culpas, Laurencio?
A pura imaginación
del alto merecimiento
de tus prendas, aprendí
el que tú dices que tengo.
Por hablarte supe hablar,
vencida de tus requiebros;
por leer en tus papeles,
libros difíciles leo;   2470
para responderte escribo.
No te tenido otro maestro
que amor; amor me ha enseñado.
Tú eres la ciencia que aprendo.
¿De qué te quejas de mí?

LAURENCIO   De mi desdicha me quejo;
pero, pues ya sabes tanto,
dame, señora, un remedio.

FINEA   El remedio es fácil.

LAURENCIO   ¿Cómo?

FINEA   Si, porque mi rudo ingenio,   2480
que todos aborrecían,
se ha transformado en discreto,
Liseo me quiere bien,
con volver a ser tan necio
como primero le tuve,
me aborrecerá Liseo.

LAURENCIO   Pues, ¿sabrás fingirte boba?

FINEA   Sí; que lo fui mucho tiempo,
y el lugar donde se nace
saben andarle los ciegos.   2490
Demás desto, las mujeres
naturaleza tenemos
tan pronta para fingir
o con amor o con miedo,
qué, antes de nacer, fingimos.

LAURENCIO   ¿Antes de nacer?

LAURENCIO   Can you pretend to be a nitwit?

FINEA   Certainly! I was a booby long enough! Just as the blind can find
            their way about the house where they grew up. Furthermore,
            even before we were born we women were disposed to pretence
            in love as well as in fear.

LAURENCIO   Before you were born?

FINEA   Haven't you ever heard that one? Listen.

LAURENCIO   I'm all ears.

FINEA   When we're in our mothers' wombs we deceive our fathers by
            pretending to be boys. They run about, happily preparing for
            our arrival with love and care and with many presents for the
            coming heir, and then out pops a girl and breaks the line of
            succession! So if they hope for a boy and get a girl, we begin
            dissembling before we were born.

LAURENCIO   A clever argument, certainly. But we'll see how well you pretend
            in this other change of such extremes.

FINEA   Careful! Here comes Liseo.

LAURENCIO   I'll hide here.

FINEA   Hurry.

LAURENCIO   Pedro, follow me.

PEDRO   You're courting danger.

LAURENCIO   In these straits what difference does it make?

SCENE XI

[Laurencio and Pedro hide; Liseo and Turín enter.]

LISEO   It's settled, at last!

TURÍN   Heaven's ordained that, in the end, she would be your wife.

FINEA	Yo pienso	
	que en tu vida lo has oído.	
	Escucha.	
LAURENCIO	Ya escucho atento.	
FINEA	Cuando estamos en el vientre	
	de nuestras madres, hacemos	2500
	entender a nuestros padres,	
	para engañar sus deseos,	
	que somos hijos varones;	
	y así verás que, contentos,	
	acuden a sus antojos	
	con amores, con requiebros,	
	y esperando el mayorazgo	
	tras tantos regalos hechos,	
	sale una hembra que corta	
	la esperanza del suceso.	2510
	Según esto, si pensaron	
	que era varón, y hembra vieron,	
	antes de nacer fingimos.	
LAURENCIO	Es evidente argumento;	
	pero yo veré si sabes	
	hacer, Finea, tan presto	
	mudanza de extremos tales.	
FINEA	Paso, que viene Liseo.	
LAURENCIO	Allí me voy a esconder.	
FINEA	Ve presto.	
LAURENCIO	Sígueme, Pedro.	2520
PEDRO	En muchos peligros andas.	
LAURENCIO	Tal estoy, que no los siento.	

[Escóndanse Laurencio y Pedro.]

ESCENA XI

[Entre Liseo con Turín.—Finea]

LISEO	En fin, queda concertado.	
TURÍN	En fin, estaba del cielo	
	que fuese tu esposa.	
LISEO	[Aparte] (Aquí	
	está mi primero dueño.)	
	¿No sabéis, señora mía,	
	cómo ha tratado Miseno	
	casar a Düardo y Nise,	
	y cómo yo también quiero	2530

LISEO	*[Aside]* And here's the master of my soul! Have you heard, m'lady? Miseno has contracted a marriage between Duardo and Nise, and I've requested that our wedding should be held with theirs.
FINEA	I don't believe you. Nise's told me that she is married secretly to you.
LISEO	To me?
FINEA	Was it you? Or was it Don Juan? Which one are you, now?
LISEO	Could such a change be possible?
FINEA	Who'd you say? It slips my mind. And if you think changes are marvelous what of the new moon that appears in the heavens every month?
LISEO	God deliver me! What is this?
TURÍN	A recurrence of her former malady.
FINEA	Now you tell me, if we have a new moon every month, where do they all go? What's happened to the old ones? Give up?
LISEO	*[Aside]* She's been mad all along!
FINEA	They use the old ones to patch up the new ones that are born waning. You're not very smart, are you?
LISEO	Lady, I'm amazed! Yesterday you—you displayed such wit.
FINEA	Well, sir, today it keeps pace with yours. It's a sign of wit to change with the times.
LISEO	So spoke the sage.
PEDRO	*[Hidden]* Into the ear of the greatest idiot.
LISEO	You've robbed me of my pleasure.
FINEA	I never laid a hand on it! Look and see if you dropped it somewhere.
LISEO	*[Aside]* What luck! I no sooner ask Octavio for her hand and come to give her the news, than I find she's reverted to her

que se hagan nuestras bodas
con las suyas?

FINEA   No lo creo;
que Nise me ha dicho a mí
que está casada en secreto
con vos.

LISEO   ¿Conmigo?

FINEA   No sé
si érades vos u Oliveros.
¿Quién sois vos?

LISEO   ¿Hay tal mudanza?

FINEA   ¿Quién decís, que no me acuerdo?
Y si mudanza os parece,
¿cómo no veis que en el cielo   2540
cada mes hay nuevas lunas?

LISEO   ¡Válgame el cielo! ¿Qué es esto?

TURÍN   ¿Si le vuelve el mal pasado?

FINEA   Pues, decidme: si tenemos
luna nueva cada mes,
¿adónde están? ¿Qué se han hecho
las viejas de tantos años?
¿Daisos por vencido?

LISEO   *[Aparte]*   Temo
que era locura su mal.

FINEA   Guárdanlas para remiendos   2550
de las que salen menguadas.
¡Veis ahí que sois un necio!

LISEO   Señora, mucho me admiro
de que ayer tan alto ingenio
mostrásedes.

FINEA   Pues, señor,
agora ha llegado al vuestro;
que la mayor discreción
es acomodarse al tiempo.

LISEO   Eso dijo el mayor sabio.

PEDRO   *[Aparte]*
Y esto escucha el mayor necio.   2560

LISEO   Quitado me habéis el gusto.

FINEA   No he tocado a vos, por cierto;
mirad que se habrá caído.

LISEO   *[Aparte]*
(¡Linda ventura tenemos!

former self! M'lady, come to your senses. Think! I acknowledge you as my master forever!

FINEA You mean mistress, silly!

LISEO Is this the way you treat a slave who pledges you his soul?

FINEA How's that?

LISEO I pledge you my soul.

FINEA What's a soul?

LISEO Soul? The governor of the body.

FINEA What's it look like?

LISEO M'lady, as a philosopher, I can only define it, not paint it.

FINEA Aren't souls the things that Saint Michael is always weighing on his scales in the paintings down at the church?

LISEO Just like the angels. Even though they are insubstantial spirits, we paint souls with bodies, and sometimes wings.

FINEA Do souls talk?

LISEO The soul operates through its instruments, through the senses and the various members of the body, that is, if it is to be efficient.

FINEA The soul's a fish?!

TURÍN She's wearing you down.

LISEO If this isn't madness, what is it?

TURÍN Fools don't go mad, sir.

LISEO Who does then?

TURÍN Wise men, sir! The diversity of their learning dizzies them into it!

LISEO Oh, Turín, I'm going back to Nise! I prefer reason even if it lacks affection. Lady, my attempt to tender you my soul has foundered. Good day.

	Pídole a Otavio a Finea,	
	y cuando a decirle vengo	
	el casamiento tratado,	
	hallo que a su ser se ha vuelto.)	
	Volved, mi señora, en vos,	
	considerando que os quiero	2570
	por mi dueño para siempre.	
FINEA	¡Por mi dueña, majadero!	
LISEO	¿Así tratáis un esclavo	
	que os da el alma?	
FINEA	¿Cómo es eso?	
LISEO	Que os doy el alma.	
FINEA	¿Qué es alma?	
LISEO	¿Alma? El gobierno del cuerpo.	
FINEA	¿Cómo es un alma?	
LISEO	Señora,	
	como filósofo puedo	
	difinirla, no pintarla.	
FINEA	¿No es alma la que en el peso	2580
	le pintan a San Miguel?	
LISEO	También a un ángel ponemos	
	alas y cuerpo, y, en fin,	
	es un espíritu bello.	
FINEA	¿Hablan las almas?	
LISEO	Las almas	
	obran por los instrumentos,	
	por los sentidos y partes	
	de que se organiza el cuerpo.	
FINEA	¿Longaniza come el alma? . . .	
TURÍN	¿En qué te cansas?	
LISEO	No puedo	2590
	pensar sino que es locura.	
TURÍN	Pocas veces de los necios	
	se hacen los locos, señor.	
LISEO	Pues, ¿de quién?	
TURÍN	De los discretos;	
	porque de diversas causas	
	nacen efetos diversos.	
LISEO	¡Ay, Turín! Vuélvome a Nise.	
	Más quiero el entendimiento	
	que toda la voluntad.	
	Señora, pues mi deseo,	2600

FINEA   I'm afraid of souls because, of the three kinds you see painted, instead of the one in purgatory or heaven, it may turn out to be the one in hell! On All Souls' Night I'm so frightened that I won't stick my head out from underneath the covers.

TURÍN   But, sir, she's the exception to my rule: a fool gone mad! They're the worst!

LISEO   I'm going to tell her father.   *[Liseo and Turín leave.]*

SCENE XII

LAURENCIO   May I come out?

FINEA   Well, how was that?

LAURENCIO   The best solution ever invented!

FINEA   Good. But I didn't like becoming a nitwit again, even in fun. If I felt that way while pretending, how could real nitwits stand to live the way they do?

LAURENCIO   By not feeling.

PEDRO   If a booby could see his reason reflected in a mirror, he'd run away from himself. They're content because they believe they are intelligent.

FINEA   Oh, speak to me, Laurencio! Speak subtly! I need to rinse my mind of stupidity!

SCENE XIII

[Nise and Celia enter.]

NISE   Always together! They must be in love; there's no other explanation.

CELIA   I'm sure they're planning to deceive you.

NISE   We can listen to them from here.

	que era de daros el alma,	
	no pudo tener efeto,	
	quedad con Dios.	
FINEA	Soy medrosa	
	de las almas, porque temo	
	que de tres que andan pintadas,	
	puede ser la del infierno.	
	La noche de los difuntos	
	no saco de puro miedo	
	la cabeza de la ropa.	
TURÍN	Ella es loca sobre necio,	2610
	que es la peor guarnición.	
LISEO	Decirlo a su padre quiero. *[Váyanse.]*	

ESCENA XII

[Laurencio y Pedro.—Finea]

LAURENCIO	¿Puedo salir? . . .	
FINEA	¿Qué te dice?	
LAURENCIO	Que ha sido el mejor remedio	
	que pudiera imaginarse.	
FINEA	Sí; pero siento, en extremo,	
	volverme a boba, aun fingida.	
	Y, pues fingida lo siento,	
	los que son bobos de veras,	
	¿cómo viven?	
LAURENCIO	No sintiendo.	2620
PEDRO	Pues si un tonto ver pudiera	
	su entendimiento a un espejo,	
	¿no fuera huyendo de sí?	
	La razón de estar contentos	
	es aquella confianza	
	de tenerse por discretos	
FINEA	Háblame, Laurencio mío,	
	sutilmente, porque quiero	
	desquitarme de ser boba.	

ESCENA XIII

[Entren Nise y Celia.—Dichos]

NISE	Siempre Finea y Laurencio	2630
	juntos. Sin duda se tienen	
	amor. No es posible menos.	

LAURENCIO	Even though my soul outstripped itself, what could it reveal to you that would equal the desires of my love? You possess my senses; choose your subtleties. Pretend that it's springtime and you're strolling through a pleasant field gathering flowers. For just so, my desires flower in my imagination and in my thoughts of you.
NISE	Are those the compliments of a brother-in-law? They sound more like lover's endearments!
CELIA	Compliments, surely, but I wouldn't want so complimentary a brother-in-law.
FINEA	Would to God that I might someday possess those senses!
LAURENCIO	What lies beyond the reach of love's challenge?
PEDRO	Your sister's eavesdropping.
LAURENCIO	Good God!
FINEA	Back to the booby!
LAURENCIO	That's it!
FINEA	Go away!
NISE	Wait! Not so fast!
LAURENCIO	I suppose you are jealous.
NISE	Jealousy is made of suspicions, but facts define treachery.
LAURENCIO	How quickly you jump to conclusions and resort to deceit! You're searching for some excuse to love Liseo who seems to be hovering ever closer to your person and your marriage! Well done, Nise, very well done! Stir up lies against me so that I'll be blamed for this wedding of yours. If you want to get married, do so, but leave me alone! *[Laurencio leaves.]*
NISE	Well turned! I came to complain of you but you complain of me! You never let me speak!
PEDRO	My master's right! Get married and make an end of it!
	[Pedro leaves.]

CELIA	Yo sospecho que te engañan.
NISE	Desde aquí los escuchemos.
LAURENCIO	¿Qué puede, hermosa Finea,
	decirte el alma, aunque sale
	de sí misma, que se iguale
	a lo que mi amor desea?

           Allá mis sentidos tienes:
escoge de lo sutil,   2640
presumiendo que en abril
por amenos prados vienes.
           Corta las diversas flores,
porque en mi imaginación,
tales los deseos son.

NISE	Éstos, Celia, ¿son amores,
	o regalos de cuñado?
CELIA	Regalos deben de ser;
	pero no quisiera ver
	cuñado tan regalado.

                                    2650

FINEA	¡Ay Dios; si llegase día
	en que viese mi esperanza
	su posesión!
LAURENCIO	¿Qué no alcanza
	una amorosa porfía?
PEDRO	Tu hermana, escuchando.
LAURENCIO	¡Ay cielos!
FINEA	Vuélvome a boba.
LAURENCIO	Eso importa.
FINEA	Vete.
NISE	Espérate, reporta
	los pasos.
LAURENCIO	¿Vendrás con celos?
NISE	Celos son para sospechas;
	traiciones son las verdades.

                                    2660

LAURENCIO	¡Qué presto te persüades
	y de engaños te aprovechas!

           ¿Querrás buscar ocasión
para querer a Liseo,
a quien ya tan cerca veo
de tu boda y posesión?
           Bien haces, Nise; haces bien.
Levántame un testimonio,
porque deste matrimonio
a mí la culpa me den.   2670

SCENE XIV

NISE   What is this?

CELIA   Pedro has fled in the same humor, which makes him as vile as
              his master.

NISE   I loathe him! Despise him! And much good I got by complaining!
              That was a wonderful stroke, to be the first to start a quarrel!

CELIA   And Pedro! Did you see the way he swaggered out?

NISE   *[To Finea]* And you! Concealing your treason while your heart is
              aflame with deceits that are burning me to death! How like a
              siren, half fish, half woman, changing from beast to woman in
              order to hurt me! Do you think you're going to have him?

FINEA   You never in your life gave me a fish or a siren, nor did we ever
              go swimming together! Oh, go on, Nise, you're acting crazy.

NISE   What's this?

CELIA   Her wit's no longer fit.

NISE   Fit or unfit, be sure of one thing: I'm so furious I could tear
              your heart out!

FINEA   You'll have to buy indulgences if you do. Think about that!

NISE   I consider your treason, a fig for your pardon! You were plot-
              ting to rob me of the soul for which my soul exists. Treacher-
              ous sister, give me back that soul which nourishes mine! You
              must be learned indeed, if you're able to disarm my soul.

FINEA   You all keep asking me for your souls, upon my soul, as if I
              were some sort of spiritual cupboard. I'm all thefts and rob-
              beries! Plunk me down in Eden and call me a serpent!

NISE   Enough of the cuckoo! Give me back my soul!

SCENE XV

[Octavio enters with Feniso and Duardo.]

OCTAVIO   What's this?

	Y si te quieres casar, déjame a mí. *[Vase.]*
NISE	¡Bien me dejas! ¡Vengo a quejarme, y te quejas! ¿Aun no me dejas hablar?
PEDRO	Tiene razón mi señor. Cásate, y acaba ya. *[Vase.]*

ESCENA XIV

NISE   ¿Qué es aquesto?

CELIA   Que se va
Pedro con el mismo humor,
   y aquí viene bien que Pedro
es tan ruin como su amo.   2680

NISE   Ya le aborrezco y desamo.
¡Qué bien con las quejas medro!
   Pero fue linda invención
anticiparse a reñir.

CELIA   Y el Pedro, ¿quién le vio ir
tan bellaco y socarrón?

NISE   Y tú, que disimulando
estás la traición que has hecho,
lleno de engaños el pecho
con que me estás abrasando,   2690
   pues, como sirena, fuiste
medio pez, medio mujer,
pues de animal a saber
para mi daño veniste,
   ¿piensas que le has de gozar?

FINEA   ¿Tú me has dado pez a mí,
ni sirena, ni yo fui
jamás contigo a la mar?
   ¡Anda, Nise, que estás loca!

NISE   ¿Qué es esto?

CELIA   A tonta se vuelve.   2700

NISE   ¡A una cosa te resuelve!
Tanto el furor me provoca,
   que el alma te he de sacar.

FINEA   ¿Tienes cuenta de perdón?

NISE   Téngola de tu traición;
pero no de perdonar.
   ¿El alma piensas quitarme
en quien el alma tenía?

FINEA	They keep asking me for their souls as though I were purgatory itself.
NISE	You are!
FINEA	Then get out if you can!
OCTAVIO	Tell me what upsets you!
FINEA	It's Nise, who, in a fit of reason, claims the unreasonable, asking me to give back all kinds of things like souls, sirens, and fishes that she swears she gave me.
OCTAVIO	Has she become a booby again?
NISE	Yes.
OCTAVIO	You're the one who addles her!
FINEA	And she's given me cause! She's stealing something that belongs to me!
OCTAVIO	Deliver me! She's mad again!
FENISO	That's life all over!
DUARDO	But weren't they just saying that she was quite bright?
OCTAVIO	Oh, God!
NISE	May I speak plainly?
OCTAVIO	Do, please!
NISE	All your worry will be ended if you command—since as a father you may command anything, but this most of all, and your honor depends on it—that Laurencio be forbidden entry to this house.
OCTAVIO	Why, pray?
NISE	Because he's the one who has caused the delay in Finea's wedding and has made me annoy you.
OCTAVIO	No sooner said than done.
NISE	And the sooner done, the better.

Dame el alma que solía,
traidora hermana, animarme.   2710
    Mucho debes de saber,
pues del alma me desalmas.

FINEA   Todos me piden sus almas:
almario debo de ser.
    Toda soy hurtos y robos.
Montes hay donde no hay gente:
yo me iré a meter serpiente.

NISE   Que ya no es tiempo de bobos.
    ¡Dame el alma!

ESCENA XV

[Otavio con Feniso y Duardo.—Dichas]

OTAVIO   ¿Qué es aquesto?

FINEA   Almas me piden a mí;   2720
¿soy yo Purgatorio?

NISE   ¡Sí!

FINEA   Pues procura salir presto.

OTAVIO   ¿No sabremos la ocasión
de vuestro enojo?

FINEA   Querer,
Nise, a fuerza de saber,
pedir lo que no es razón.
    Almas, sirenas y peces
dice que me ha dado a mí.

OTAVIO   ¿Hase vuelto a boba?

NISE   Sí.

OTAVIO   Tú pienso que la embobeces.   2730

FINEA   Ella me ha dado ocasión;
que me quita lo que es mío.

OTAVIO   Se ha vuelto a su desvarío.
¡Muerto soy!

FENISO   Desdichas son.

DUARDO   ¿No decían que ya estaba
con mucho seso?

OTAVIO   ¡Ay de mí!

NISE   Yo quiero hablar claro.

OTAVIO   Di.

NISE   Todo tu daño se acaba
    con mandar resueltamente

Scene XVI

[Pedro and Laurencio enter.]

PEDRO   You seem to be happy.

LAURENCIO   It was a marvelous idea.

CELIA   Here comes Laurencio now!

OCTAVIO   When I built this house, Laurencio, I had no intention of found-
             ing an academy. When I taught Nise to read and write it was so
             that she might become a prudent woman; it was not my inten-
             tion she become a poet! I've always been of the opinion that
             moderate intelligence was all that was needed to guarantee a
             prudent woman her share of learning. I want no more poems! I
             silence the songs! The sonnets will cease! My days are numbered
             and I want to enjoy what's left. If you cannot afford gifts of sub-
             stance, go woo some other maiden with your verses! The great-
             est poetry is both silent and golden. Even the great Garcilaso can
             be bought for a couple of coppers; and he has written so many
             profound and elegant sonnets you couldn't even begin to match
             them! You are not welcome here as long as you suffer from this
             disease of poesy. And so, with this warning, go with God.

LAURENCIO   Very well, provided you give me my bride. It's only just that
             you do as you please in your home, but I should be able to do
             the same in mine.

OCTAVIO   What bride?

LAURENCIO   Finea.

OCTAVIO   You're mad!

LAURENCIO   There are present three witnesses to the consent that she gave
             me over a month ago.

OCTAVIO   And who may they be?

LAURENCIO   Duardo, Feniso, and Pedro.

OCTAVIO   Is this true?

FENISO   Octavio, she gave it to him of her own free will.

—pues, como padre, podrás,   2740
y, aunque en todo, en esto más,
pues tu honor no lo consiente—,
    que Laurencio no entre aquí.

OTAVIO   ¿Por qué?

NISE   Porque él ha causado
que ésta no se haya casado
y que yo te enoje a ti.

OTAVIO   Pues, ¡eso es muy fácil cosa!

NISE   Pues tu casa en paz tendrás.

ESCENA XVI

[Salen Pedro y Laurencio.—Dichos]

PEDRO   ¡Contento, en efeto, estás!

LAURENCIO ¡Invención maravillosa!   2750

CELIA   Ya Laurencio viene aquí.

OTAVIO   Laurencio, cuando labré
esta casa, no pensé
que academia instituí;
    ni cuando a Nise crïaba
pensé que para poeta,
sino que a mujer perfeta,
con las letras la enseñaba.
    Siempre alabé la opinión
de que a la mujer prudente,   2760
con saber medianamente,
le sobra la discreción.
    No quiero más poesías:
los sonetos se acabaron,
y las músicas cesaron;
que son ya breves mis días.
    Por allá los podréis dar,
si os faltan telas y rasos;
que no hay tales Garcilasos
como dinero y callar.   2770
    Éste venden por dos reales,
y tiene tantos sonetos,
elegantes y discretos,
que vos no los haréis tales.
    Ya no habéis de entrar aquí
con este achaque. Id con Dios.

LAURENCIO Es muy justo, como vos
me deis a mi esposa a mí;
    que vos hacéis vuestro gusto

DUARDO   It's the truth.

PEDRO   Wasn't it enough for my master to say so?

OCTAVIO   Her word, given at a time when she was a nitwit and to a man
            who was deceiving her, doesn't count. Tell me, Finea, are you a
            nitwit?

FINEA   When I choose to be.

OCTAVIO   And when you don't?

FINEA   Then I'm not.

OCTAVIO   What am I waiting for? Since she's no longer a nitwit, she'll be
            married to Liseo. I'm off to the judge.   *[Octavio leaves.]*

NISE   Come, Celia, follow him! I'm as desperate as I'm jealous.

                              [Nise and Celia leave.]

LAURENCIO   In God's name, follow him! The two of you! Protect my interests.

FENISO   Our friendship demands it.

DUARDO   By God, he was ill-advised.

FENISO   You talk as if you were already Nise's husband.

DUARDO   I plan to be.

                              [Duardo and Feniso leave.]

SCENE XVII

LAURENCIO   All's lost. Nise told him of our love. What can be done if I may
            no longer come to see you?

FINEA   Stay here.

LAURENCIO   Where?

FINEA   I can hide you.

LAURENCIO   But where?

FINEA   There is a loft in this house that's a perfect hiding place.

en vuestra casa, y es bien   2780
que en la mía yo también
haga lo que fuere justo.

OTAVIO   ¿Qué mujer os tengo yo?

LAURENCIO   Finea.

OTAVIO   ¿Estás loco?

LAURENCIO   Aquí
hay tres testigos del *sí*
que ha más de un mes que me dio.

OTAVIO   ¿Quién son?

LAURENCIO   Duardo, Feniso
y Pedro.

OTAVIO   ¿Es esto verdad?

FENISO   Ella, de su voluntad,
Otavio, dársele quiso.   2790

DUARDO   Así es verdad.

PEDRO   ¿No bastaba
que mi señor lo dijese?

OTAVIO   Que, como simple, le diese
a un hombre que la engañaba,
    no ha de valer. Di, Finea:
¿no eres simple?

FINEA   Cuando quiero.

OTAVIO   ¿Y cuando no?

FINEA   No.

OTAVIO   ¿Qué espero?
Mas, cuando simple no sea,
    con Liseo está casada.
A la Justicia me voy.   [*Váyase Otavio.*]   2800

NISE   Ven, Celia, tras él; que estoy
celosa y desesperada.

                        [*Y váyanse Nise y Celia.*]

LAURENCIO   ¡Id, por Dios, tras él los dos!
No me suceda un disgusto.

FENISO   Por vuestra amistad es justo.

DUARDO   ¡Mal hecho ha sido, por Dios!

FENISO   ¿Ya habláis como desposado
de Nise?

DUARDO   Piénsolo ser.

                        [*Y váyanse Duardo y Feniso.*]

[Enter Clara.]

CLARA   M'lady?

FINEA   You hold my fate in your hands. Take Laurencio to the loft, and
             with the utmost secrecy!

CLARA   And Pedro?

FINEA   Take him too.

CLARA   Gentlemen, forward march!

LAURENCIO   I swear to you, I'm trembling!

FINEA   Whatever for?

PEDRO   Clara, when supper comes along, remind your mistress to save
             us a little something.

CLARA   There'll be others in this house who'll eat worse than you.

PEDRO   Off to the attic I go like a cat!

                        [Laurencio, Pedro, and Clara leave.]

SCENE XVIII

FINEA   Having openly declared my love, why should I treat it as
             impossible? There is nothing more painful and scandalous for
             an honest woman than to have her lover discovered. The best
             of love is had in secret.

SCENE XIX

[Octavio enters.]

OCTAVIO   [Aside] I'll do it even though I have every right to vent my anger.

FINEA   Have you calmed down?

OCTAVIO   Persuaded by the others.

ESCENA XVII

LAURENCIO   Todo se ha echado a perder;
            Nise mi amor le ha contado.   2810
                ¿Qué remedio puede haber,
            si a verte no puedo entrar?

FINEA   No salir.

LAURENCIO   ¿Dónde he de estar?

FINEA   ¿Yo no te sabré esconder?

LAURENCIO   ¿Dónde?

FINEA   En casa hay un desván
            famoso para esconderte.
            ¡Clara!

            [Entre Clara.]

CLARA   ¡Mi señora!

FINEA   Advierte
            que mis desdichas están
                en tu mano. Con secreto
            lleva a Laurencio al desván.   2820

CLARA   ¿Y a Pedro?

FINEA   También.

CLARA   Galán,
            camine.

LAURENCIO   Yo te prometo
            que voy temblando.

FINEA   ¿De qué?

PEDRO   Clara, en llegando la hora
            de muquir, di a tu señora
            que algún sustento nos dé.

CLARA   Otro comerá peor
            que tú.

PEDRO   ¿Yo al desván? ¿Soy gato?

            [Váyanse Laurencio, Pedro y Clara.]

ESCENA XVIII

FINEA   ¿Por qué de imposible trato,
            este mi público amor?   2830
                En llegándose a saber
            una voluntad, no hay cosa
            más triste y escandalosa

FINEA	I beg a thousand pardons.
OCTAVIO	And Laurencio?
FINEA	He's sworn here to leave the court, forever!
OCTAVIO	Where has he gone?
FINEA	Up to Toledo.
OCTAVIO	Well done.
FINEA	Never fear. He won't return to Madrid.
OCTAVIO	Daughter, born a simpleton, by some miracle of love you were transformed. How could you suffer such a lapse?
FINEA	What did you expect? Never trust a nitwit.
OCTAVIO	Well, I'll remedy that.
FINEA	Pray, why, since he's gone away?
OCTAVIO	Men deceive you altogether too easily. Henceforth, whenever you see one, I want you to hide yourself so that no man will ever behold you again.
FINEA	Hide? Where?
OCTAVIO	In some secret place.
FINEA	What about the attic, the loft where the cats are? Should I hide there?
OCTAVIO	Wherever you like, so long as they don't see you.
FINEA	Very well, the loft it is. You've ordered it, so it must be right, but remember, you ordered it.
OCTAVIO	Yes, yes, yes, a thousand times YES!

SCENE XX

[Liseo and Turín enter.]

LISEO	Having loved Nise so ardently, I can't have forgotten her completely.

   para una honrada mujer.
    Lo que tiene de secreto,
   esto tiene amor de gusto.

ESCENA XIX

[Entre Otavio.—Finea]

OTAVIO   *[Aparte]*
     Harélo, aunque fuera justo
     poner mi enojo en efeto.

FINEA   ¿Vienes ya desenojado?

OTAVIO   Por los que me lo han pedido.   2840

FINEA   Perdón mil veces te pido.

OTAVIO   ¿Y Laurencio?

FINEA   Aquí ha jurado
     no entrar en la Corte más.

OTAVIO   ¿A dónde se fue?

FINEA   A Toledo.

OTAVIO   ¡Bien hizo!

FINEA   No tengas miedo
     que vuelva a Madrid jamás.

OTAVIO   Hija, pues simple naciste,
     y por milagros de amor
     dejaste el pasado error,
     ¿cómo el ingenio perdiste?   2850

FINEA   Qué quiere, padre? A la fe,
     de bobos no hay que fiar.

OTAVIO   Yo lo pienso remediar.

FINEA   ¿Cómo, si el otro se fue?

OTAVIO   Pues te engañan fácilmente
     los hombres, en viendo alguno,
     te has de esconder; que ninguno
     te ha de ver eternamente.

FINEA   Pues, ¿dónde?

OTAVIO   En parte secreta.

FINEA   ¿Será bien en un desván,   2860
     donde los gatos están?
     ¿Quieres tú que allí me meta?

OTAVIO   Adonde te diere gusto,
     como ninguno te vea.

FINEA	There are men coming! I must hide! I'm off to the loft, father!
OCTAVIO	Liseo doesn't count, child!
FINEA	To the loft, Father! There are men!
OCTAVIO	Don't you understand? They're guests!
FINEA	You can't go wrong if you obey! No man will ever see me again unless he be my husband! To the loft! *[Exit Finea.]*

Scene XXI

LISEO	I've heard of your troubles.
OCTAVIO	A father's lot.
LISEO	But you can set them right.
OCTAVIO	I've already done so by expelling one of those who are upsetting my home.
LISEO	How so?
OCTAVIO	Laurencio has left for Toledo.
LISEO	Well done!
OCTAVIO	And do you plan to stay on here without getting married? Your presence here gives rise to the very same disturbances. You have kept me dangling with words, Liseo, for two whole months!
LISEO	Try to understand my predicament! Forced by my parents, I come here to marry Finea, and I find her to be a perfect simpleton. And now, Octavio, you persist in forcing me to want her?
OCTAVIO	You're right, it's settled! However, she's neat and lovely, and owns enough doubloons to double a bar of steel in two! Did you expect forty thousand ducats and a phoenix to boot? Is Finea lame? Or blind? And even if she were, is there any imperfection of nature that cannot be shaved away with a golden razor?

FINEA   Pues, ¡alto! En el desván sea;
                 tú lo mandas, será justo.
                     Y advierte que lo has mandado.

OTAVIO   ¡Una y mil veces!

ESCENA XX

[Entren Liseo y Turín.—Dichos]

LISEO   Si quise
                 con tantas veras a Nise,
                 mal puedo haberla olvidado.   2870

FINEA   Hombres vienen. Al desván,
                 padre, yo voy a esconderme.

OTAVIO   Hija, Liseo no importa.

FINEA   Al desván, padre: hombres vienen.

OTAVIO   Pues, ¿no ves que son de casa?

FINEA   No yerra quien obedece.
                 No me ha de ver hombre más,
                 sino quien mi esposo fuere.   *[Váyase Finea.]*

ESCENA XXI

LISEO   Tus disgustos he sabido.

OTAVIO   Soy padre . . .

LISEO   Remedio puedes   2880
                 poner en aquestas cosas.

OTAVIO   Ya le he puesto, con que dejen
                 mi casa los que la inquietan.

LISEO   Pues, ¿de qué manera?

OTAVIO   Fuese
                 Laurencio a Toledo ya.

LISEO   ¡Qué bien has hecho!

OTAVIO   ¿Y tú crees
                 vivir aquí, sin casarte?
                 Porque el mismo inconveniente
                 se sigue de que aquí estés.
                 Hoy hace, Liseo, dos meses   2890
                 que me traes en palabras.

LISEO   ¡Bien mi término agradeces!
                 Vengo a casar con Finea,
                 forzado de mis parientes,
                 y hallo una simple mujer.
                 ¿Que la quiera, Otavio, quieres?

LISEO	Give me Nise.

OCTAVIO Not more than two hours ago, Miseno promised her to Duardo in my name! I tell you clearly that you have until tomorrow to think it over. Unless you decide to marry Finea, never again enter this house—which you've already set in an uproar— you—you—POET! *[Octavio leaves.]*

SCENE XXII

LISEO What do you make of that?

TURÍN Bend with the wind and marry Finea. If it's worth twenty thousand to suffer an idiot, they're giving you an extra twenty. And if you don't marry her there'll be more than seven who'll cry "What idiocy!"

LISEO My aversion to fools gives me the courage not to marry a nitwit! Let's be off!

TURÍN The suitor with little in his purse who incurs debts as large as yours is not much wittier than the nitwit he rejects.

SCENE XXIII

[They leave and Finea and Clara enter.]

FINEA So far, so good.

CLARA Don't worry about being discovered.

FINEA How my senses develop under the tutelage of my love!

CLARA And the patience with which the dear waits up there in the loft!

FINEA Poor Laurencio, but what better place for love than a lofty one?

CLARA Born into these giddy times we're all living quite loftily!

FINEA Except for the very humble who never rise.

OTAVIO	Tienes razón. ¡Acabóse!
	Pero es limpia, hermosa, y tiene
	tanto doblón que podría
	doblar el mármol más fuerte. 2900
	¿Querías cuarenta mil
	ducados con una Fénix?
	¿Es coja o manca Finea?
	¿Es ciega? Y, cuando lo fuese,
	¿hay falta en Naturaleza
	que con oro no se afeite?

| LISEO | Dame a Nise. |

OTAVIO	No ha dos horas
	que Miseno la promete
	a Düardo, en nombre mío;
	y, pues hablo claramente, 2910
	hasta mañana a estas horas
	te doy para que lo pienses;
	porque, de no te casar,
	para que en tu vida entres
	por las puertas de mi casa
	que tan enfadada tienes.
	Haz cuenta que eres poeta. *[Váyase Otavio.]*

ESCENA XXII

| LISEO | ¿Qué te dice? |

TURÍN	Que te aprestes,
	y con Finea te cases;
	porque si veinte mereces, 2920
	por que sufras una boba
	te añaden los otros veinte.
	Si te dejas de casar,
	te han de decir más de siete:
	«¡Miren la bobada!»

LISEO	Vamos;
	que mi temor se resuelve
	de no se casar a bobas.

TURÍN	Que se casa me parece
	a bobas, quien sin dineros
	en tanta costa se mete. *[Váyanse.]* 2930

ESCENA XXIII

[Entren Finea y Clara.]

| FINEA | Hasta agora, bien nos va. |

CLARA   By the same token the man who thinks himself better than
         Plato lodges in the loft of presumption.

FINEA   Driven there by the loftiness of Plato's reputation.

CLARA   Loftiness urges the spurned to rise above their station and the
         fool to lodge above himself.

FINEA   Have I ever told you why it's natural for nitwits to think so
         highly of themselves?

CLARA   No, why?

FINEA   Their pride robs them of all sense. When I was a booby, I held
         myself to be most discreet. Since knowledge is compatible
         with humility, now that I have some ability, I count myself
         ignorant.

CLARA   The death of the murderer's soul is something few will witness
         because he hides it in the loft of his madness. So too with those
         boors who waste their lives on a thousand witticisms and graces
         but are disgraced at every turn. And what attic antics induce a
         lady to surrender an hour of discretion and pay with a lifetime
         of disgrace? The man who thinks himself a dandy in the loft of
         his pride changes his gait to alligator; and then there's the mule
         who brays his claim to the title of a thoroughbred, the amateur
         poet in the loft sawing wooden verses, and the man who travels
         in the lofty circles of circumspection but is always in the path
         of danger. Finally—

FINEA   One moment; Father approaches.

Scene XXIV

[Enter Octavio, Miseno, Duardo, and Feniso.]

MISENO   And you told him that?

OCTAVIO   Certainly; which gives you some notion of how furious he
          made me. I swear to God I will no longer allow persons in my
          house who irritate me.

CLARA	No hayas miedo que se entienda.
FINEA	¡Oh, cuánto a mi amada prenda deben mis sentidos ya!
CLARA	¡Con la humildad que se pone en el desván . . . !
FINEA	No te espantes; que es propia casa de amantes, aunque Laurencio perdone.
CLARA	¡Y quién no vive en desván de cuantos hoy han nacido! . . .
FINEA	Algún humilde que ha sido de los que en lo bajo están.
CLARA	¡En el desván vive el hombre que se tiene por más sabio que Platón!
FINEA	Hácele agravio; que fue divino su nombre.
CLARA	¡En el desván, el que anima a grandezas su desprecio! ¡En el desván más de un necio que por discreto se estima! . . .
FINEA	¿Quieres que te diga yo cómo es falta natural de necios, no pensar mal de sí mismos?
CLARA	¿Cómo no?
FINEA	La confianza secreta tanto el sentido les roba, que, cuando era yo muy boba, me tuve por muy discreta; y como es tan semejante el saber con la humildad, ya que tengo habilidad, me tengo por ignorante.

CLARA	¡En el desván vive bien
	un matador criminal,
	cuya muerte natural
	ninguno o pocos la ven!
	   ¡En el desván, de mil modos,
	y sujeto a mil desgracias,
	aquél que diciendo gracias
	es desgraciado con todos!
	   ¡En el desván, una dama
	que, creyendo a quien la inquieta,

2940

2950

2960

2970

FENISO	You are absolutely right in getting rid of all those irksome boys.
OCTAVIO	He had the audacity to ask for Nise's hand! I told him never again to think of such a thing! The matter's settled!
MISENO	One moment; here is Finea.
OCTAVIO	Daughter, listen.
FINEA	Willingly, when you're alone, for such was your command and—
OCTAVIO	One moment! Finea, I've given your hand in marriage to—
CLARA	Oh! Such language! To use the word "marriage" with men present!
OCTAVIO	What is this?! Do you think I'm mad?
FINEA	No, Father, but there are men present! And I'm off to the loft!
OCTAVIO	Daughter, they are here in all good will!
FENISO	And I, particularly, that you may do with me what you will.
FINEA	Good heavens! Don't you know what my father's commanded?!
MISENO	Listen a moment. We've agreed upon your wedding.
FINEA	Oh, that's good, that is! However, there will never be a daughter more obedient than I. I'm off to the loft!
MISENO	Don't you find Feniso attractive?
FINEA	To the loft, sir, I'm off to the loft!

[Finea and Clara leave.]

SCENE XXV

DUARDO	Why did you tell her to hide herself from men?
OCTAVIO	By all that's holy, I don't know how to answer you! I'm angry with her! . . . and out of sorts with my stars.

por una hora de discreta,
pierde mil años de fama!
    ¡En el desván, un preciado
de lindo, y es un caimán,
pero tiénele el desván,
como el espejo, engañado!
    ¡En el desván, el que canta
con voz de carro de bueyes,   2980
y el que viene de Muleyes
y a los godos se levanta!
    ¡En el desván, el que escribe
versos legos y donados,
y el que, por vanos cuidados,
sujeto a peligros vive!
    Finalmente . . .

FINEA   Espera un poco;
que viene mi padre aquí.

Escena XXIV

[Otavio, Miseno, Duardo, Feniso.—Dichas]

MISENO   ¿Eso le dijiste?

OTAVIO   Sí;
que a tal furor me provoco.   2990
    No ha de quedar, ¡vive el cielo!,
en mi casa quien me enoje.

FENISO   Y es justo que se despoje
de tanto necio mozuelo.

OTAVIO   Pidióme graciosamente
que con Nise le casase;
díjele que no pensase
en tal cosa eternamente,
    y así estoy determinado.

MISENO   Oíd, que está aquí Finea.   3000

OTAVIO   Hija, escucha . . .

FINEA   Cuando vea,
como me lo habéis mandado,
    que estáis solo.

OTAVIO   Espera un poco;
que te ha casado.

CLARA   ¡Que nombres
casamiento donde hay hombres! . . .

OTAVIO   Luego, ¿tenéisme por loco?

MISENO   Here comes Liseo. Settle the matter.

OCTAVIO   What can I say without her?

SCENE XXVI

[Liseo, Nise, and Turín enter.]

LISEO   Now that I take my leave of you, I want you to understand how
            much I lose in loving you.

NISE   I admit that your person is worthy of esteem, and if my
            father will only consent to make you mine, I will be yours
            entire. Vengeance has its own way of quelling lovers' quar-
            rels, doesn't it?

LISEO   Oh, Nise, would my eyes had never seen you. You set my soul
            on fire as surely as Helen set fire to Troy! I came to marry your
            sister but you assaulted my heart and stole its most precious
            jewel: its liberty. Not even gold, with a strength that can tear
            down the mountains of society, has ever been able to humble
            my thoughts and gild them with the cheap luster that so often
            blinds the mighty. Nise, I'm leaving and I hope you'll live to
            mourn my absence.

TURÍN   Lovely Nise, you've learned, I hope, to temper your disdain.
            Your love is departing by post to the roadside inn of injuries.

NISE   Turín, the tears of a single man are the surest poison known to
            woman. More women have died from the torture of your tears
            than from fire, pincers, and rack.

TURÍN   *[Indicating Liseo.]* Then behold a man who cries. Are you some
            sort of tiger? Panther? Lynx? A goblin? An owl? A—a—
            Pandorga? I'm not quite up on my mythology, but which of
            these are you?

NISE   Enough! Isn't it enough to say, "I'm conquered!"

            [Enter Celia.]

Finea	No, padre; mas hay aquí hombres, y voyme al desván.
Otavio	Aquí por tu bien están.
Feniso	Vengo a que os sirváis de mí.
Finea	¡Jesús, señor! ¿No sabéis lo que mi padre ha mandado?
Miseno	Oye; que hemos concertado que os caséis.
Finea	¡Gracia tenéis! No ha de haber hija obediente como yo. Voyme al desván.
Miseno	Pues, ¿no es Feniso galán?
Finea	¡Al desván, señor pariente!

3010

[Váyanse Finea y Clara.]

Escena XXV

Duardo	¿Cómo vos le habéis mandado que de los hombres se esconda?
Otavio	No sé, por Dios, qué os responda. Con ella estoy enojado, o con mi contraria estrella.
Miseno	Ya viene Liseo aquí. Determinaos.
Otavio	Yo, por mí, ¿qué puedo decir sin ella?

3020

Escena XXVI

[Liseo, Nise y Turín.—Dichos. Después Celia]

Liseo	Ya que me parto de ti, sólo quiero que conozcas lo que pierdo por quererte.
Nise	Conozco que tu persona merece ser estimada; y como mi padre agora venga bien en que seas mío, yo me doy por tuya toda; que en los agravios de amor es la venganza gloriosa.
Liseo	¡Ay Nise! ¡Nunca te vieran mis ojos, pues fuiste sola de mayor incendio en mí

3030

CELIA	Lady, listen!
NISE	Is that you, Celia?
CELIA	Of course!
NISE	What do you mean bursting in on us this way?
OCTAVIO	Daughter, what is this?
CELIA	Something which ought to put you on the alert! You especially!
OCTAVIO	Alert?
CELIA	Just now I saw Clara carrying a basket loaded with two partridges, two slices of ham, two rabbits, bread, napkins, knives, salt cellar, and a wine skin! I followed her and saw that she was headed for the loft.
OCTAVIO	Don't be silly, that was for her nitwit of a mistress.
FENISO	Boobies are eating well these days!
OCTAVIO	She's taken to hiding in the loft because I told her today that she should keep herself away from men in order that they may not deceive her.
CELIA	That explanation would do, had I not been curious enough to see for myself. I followed her; she closed the door!
MISENO	What of that?
CELIA	What of that? What if she spread upon the floor, as though it were a grassy slope in springtime, a large white tablecloth on which she and Finea ate heartily—in the company of two men!
OCTAVIO	Men! My honor is, indeed, in good hands! Did you recognize them?
CELIA	No.
FENISO	If you're going to spy, Celia, then for heaven's sake do it well!
OCTAVIO	It couldn't be Laurencio, he's in Toledo.

que fue Elena para Troya!   3040
Vine a casar con tu hermana,
y, en viéndote, Nise hermosa,
mi libertad salteaste,
del alma preciosa joya.
Nunca más el oro pudo
con su fuerza poderosa,
que ha derribado montañas
de costumbres generosas,
humillar mis pensamientos
a la bajeza que doran   3050
los resplandores, que a veces
ciegan tan altas personas.
Nise, ¡duélete de mí,
ya que me voy!

TURÍN   Tiempla agora,
bella Nise, tus desdenes;
que se va amor por la posta
a la casa del agravio.

NISE   Turín, las lágrimas solas
de un hombre han sido en el mundo
veneno para nosotras.   3060
No han muerto tantas mujeres
de fuego, hierro y ponzoña,
como de lágrimas vuestras.

TURÍN   Pues mira un hombre que llora.
¿Eres tú bárbara tigre?
¿Eres pantera? ¿Eres onza?
¿Eres duende? ¿Eres lechuza?
¿Eres Circe? ¿Eres Pandorga?
¿Cuál de aquestas cosas eres,
que no estoy bien en historias?   3070

NISE   ¿No basta decir que estoy
rendida?

              [Entre Celia.]

CELIA   Escucha, señora . . .

NISE   ¿Eres Celia?

CELIA   Sí.

NISE   ¿Qué quieres,
que ya todos se alborotan
de verte venir turbada?

OTAVIO   Hija, ¿qué es esto?

CELIA   Una cosa
que os ha de poner cuidado.

DUARDO   Control your rage, sir. Feniso and I will go up.

OCTAVIO   I'll make them know whose home they have affronted!

            [Octavio leaves.]

SCENE XXVII

FENISO   Pray God nothing happens!

NISE   Never fear. My father has a good head on his shoulders.

DUARDO   And good sense is the most prized of jewels.

FENISO   And ignorance, Duardo, is the greatest error. You can take pride
            in this, Nise, that in all Europe there is no one who could equal
            your brilliance.

LISEO   Which conforms with her beauty.

SCENE XXVIII

*[Enter Laurencio, Finea, Clara, and Pedro fleeing Octavio, who follows with
            sword in hand.]*

OCTAVIO   Steal my honor? I'll have your life a thousand times over!

LAURENCIO   Hold your sword! It is I—and my wife!

FENISO   Is it Laurencio?

LAURENCIO   Who does it look like?

OCTAVIO   Who else could it be?

FINEA   Well, Father, why so angry?

OCTAVIO   You villain! Didn't you tell me that that scoundrel was in
            Toledo?

Otavio	¿Cuidado?	
Celia	Yo vi que agora llevaba Clara un tabaque con dos perdices, dos lonjas, dos gazapos, pan, toallas, cuchillo, salero y bota. Seguíla, y vi que al desván caminaba . . .	3080
Otavio	Celia loca, para la boba sería.	
Feniso	¡Qué bien que comen las bobas!	
Otavio	Ha dado en irse al desván, porque hoy le dije a la tonta que, para que no la engañen, en viendo un hombre, se esconda.	3090
Celia	Eso fuera, a no haber sido para saberlo, curiosa. Subí tras ella, y cerró la puerta . . .	
Miseno	Pues bien, ¿qué importa?	
Celia	¿No importa, si en aquel suelo, como si fuera una alfombra de las que la primavera en prados fértiles borda, tendió unos blancos manteles, a quien hicieron corona dos hombres, ella y Finea?	3100
Otavio	¿Hombres? ¡Buena va mi honra! ¿Conocístelos?	
Celia	No pude.	
Feniso	Mira bien si se te antoja, Celia.	
Otavio	No será Laurencio, que está en Toledo.	
Duardo	Reporta el enojo. Yo y Feniso subiremos.	
Otavio	¡Reconozcan la casa que han afrentado! *[Váyase Otavio.]*	

Escena XXVII

Feniso	No suceda alguna cosa.	3110

FINEA	I told the truth, Father; that's exactly what we call the loft for it's awfully high! *[Pointing to Octavio]* He commanded me to hide! Well, then, he's to blame! Me, alone in the loft? He knows how frightened I become.
OCTAVIO	I'll cut out her tongue and sew up her mouth!
MISENO	There's no hope for her.
TURÍN	And what of that vixen Clara with her rabbits?
CLARA	My lady ordered them.
MISENO	Octavio, you're a wise man, and I need not remind you that there are times when cutting the the knot is no more profitable than unravelling.
OCTAVIO	Which do you advise?
MISENO	I'd unravel.
OCTAVIO	Feniso, if good intentions are tantamount to good deeds, then accept my good intentions; and you too, Duardo. However, Finea has found herself a husband, and Nise has finally taken to Liseo, while he's told me that he loves her—worships her, in fact.
FENISO	They had all the luck! Be patient, heart. Let them enjoy the fruits of their honest hopes.
LAURENCIO	My sails are full! I hereby give my hand to Finea.
OCTAVIO	Give him yours, you wily nitwit.
LISEO	And I give mine to Nise.
OCTAVIO	And you, do likewise.
LAURENCIO	My victory is well earned: for if I gave her reason, she gave me the recollection—of forty thousand ducats.
PEDRO	And what of Pedro? Couldn't I gnaw upon a bone from the table of this wedding feast?
FINEA	Clara is yours—and she's no mean bone!

NISE	No hará; que es cuerdo mi padre.
DUARDO	Cierto que es divina joya el entendimiento.
FENISO	Siempre yerra, Düardo, el que ignora. Desto os podéis alabar, Nise, pues en toda Europa no tiene igual vuestro ingenio.
LISEO	Con su hermosura conforma.

Escena XXVIII

[Salga, con la espada desnuda, Otavio siguiendo a Laurencio, Finea, Clara y Pedro.]

OTAVIO	¡Mil vidas he de quitar a quien el honor me roba!	3120
LAURENCIO	¡Detened la espada, Otavio! Yo soy, que estoy con mi esposa.	
FENISO	¿Es Laurencio?	
LAURENCIO	¿No lo veis?	
OTAVIO	¿Quién pudiera ser agora, sino Laurencio, mi infamia?	
FINEA	Pues, padre, ¿de qué se enoja?	
OTAVIO	¡Oh infame! ¿No me dijiste que el dueño de mi deshonra estaba en Toledo?	
FINEA	Padre, si aqueste desván se nombra «Toledo», verdad le dije. Alto está, pero no importa; que más lo estaba el Alcázar y la Puente de Segovia, y hubo Juanelos que a él subieron agua sin sogas. ¿Él, no me mandó esconder? Pues suya es la culpa toda. Sola en un desván, ¡mal año! Ya sabe que soy medrosa . . .	3130 3140
OTAVIO	¡Cortaréle aquella lengua! ¡Rasgaréle aquella boca!	
MISENO	Éste es caso sin remedio.	
NISE	¿Y la Clara socarrona que llevaba los gazapos?	
CLARA	Mandómelo mi señora.	

TURÍN   And I? Was I born at Trausi where they weep for the newborn
            and laugh for the dead?

NISE   Celia has always been your votary and now shall be your bride.

TURÍN   Then she shall be my buttery, booty, and bride!

FENISO   You and I are left high and dry. Give me your lovely hand.

DUARDO   If the audience, who forgives our faults, will allow it! This is an
            end, for all wise men, fit for a nitwit comedy!

THE END

Miseno	Otavio, vos sois discreto:
	ya sabéis que tanto monta
	cortar como desatar.
Otavio	¿Cuál me aconsejáis que escoja? 3150
Miseno	Desatar.
Otavio	Señor Feniso,
	si la voluntad es obra,
	recibid la voluntad.
	Y vos, Düardo, la propia;
	que Finea se ha casado,
	y Nise, en fin, se conforma
	con Liseo, que me ha dicho
	que la quiere y que la adora.
Feniso	Si fue, señor, su ventura,
	¡paciencia! Que el premio gozan 3160
	de sus justas esperanzas.
Laurencio	Todo corre viento en popa.
	¿Daré a Finea la mano?
Otavio	Dádsela, boba ingeniosa.
Liseo	¿Y yo a Nise?
Otavio	Vos también.
Laurencio	Bien merezco esta vitoria,
	pues le he dado entendimiento,
	si ella me da la memoria
	de cuarenta mil ducados.
Pedro	Y Pedro, ¿no es bien que coma 3170
	algún güeso, como perro,
	de la mesa de estas bodas?
Finea	Clara es tuya.
Turín	Y yo, ¿nací
	donde a los que nacen lloran,
	y ríen a los que mueren?
Nise	Celia, que fue tu devota,
	será tu esposa, Turín.
Turín	Mi bota será y mi novia.
Feniso	Vos y yo sólo faltamos.
	Dad acá esa mano hermosa. 3180
Duardo	Al senado la pedid,
	si nuestras faltas perdona;
	que aquí, para los discretos,
	da fin *La comedia boba*.